Celtic Rune

Heart of the Battle Series, Volume 2

Lexy Timms

Published by Dark Shadow Publishing, 2015.

CELTIC RUNE
The Heart of the Battle Series
Book 2

By
Lexy Timms

Love & College
Billionaire Heart
First Love

Heart of the Battle Series

Celtic Viking
Book 1
Celtic Rune
Book 2
Celtic Mann
Book 3
Coming June 2015

In a world plagued with darkness, she would be his salvation.

No one gave Erik a choice as to whether he would fight or not. Duty to the crown belonged to him, his father's legacy remaining beyond the grave.

Taken by the beauty of the countryside surrounding her, Linzi would do anything to protect her father's land. Britain is under attack and Scotland is next. At a time she should be focused on suitors, the men of her country have gone to war and she's left to stand alone.

Love will become available, but will passion at the touch of the enemy unravel her strong hold first?

** This is NOT Erotica. It's Romance and a love story.

* This is book 1 of a 3 book series *

Lexy Timms Newsletter:
http://eepurl.com/9i0vD
Lexy Timms Facebook Page:
https://www.facebook.com/SavingForever
Lexy Timms Website:
http://lexytimms.wix.com/savingforever

Chapter 1

Linzi

Silence surrounded her, the only sound came from the soft panting tumbling from her lips. She hovered just above the blonde, muscular stranger, the borrowed knife buried just behind his head into the hardened earth. She sat still a moment longer, assured her movements would draw him from his slumber and yet he didn't budge.

She needed a few deep breaths to still her rapidly beating heart. Linzi then carefully slipped off of his hip and leaned over for the knife, staring at the beautifully ornate handle. She pulled and pushed against it, her teeth locked tightly together as she worked the weapon free from its hold. She hadn't the courage to take the man's life, or perhaps it was more she wasn't coward enough to do it while he lay dead to the waking world. From the depth she had managed to stick the knife into the earth, she at least knew she had the strength to do it.

She straddled the injured stranger, trying to ignore the wonderful sensation of his warmth between her legs. It beckoned to be tempted further. *Nor the now*, she scolded herself. This was not the time.

Her body lurched backward as the knife released, the power of her tugging almost giving way to momentum that could roll her down the small hill behind her. She heaved a sigh, bending down to cut a small strip from her gown and wrapping the weapon in the material. She would keep it until he demanded it back or forgot he had ever had it – if he lived. Surely it was worth something in the nearby town. Treasures such as this one were far too difficult to come by. Linzi stood, turning to ensure her solitude once more before looking back toward the Saxon. He was breathtaking, her stomach tightening at the memory of the sensation of his strong hands gripping her, his hips bucking as if sex might grant him healing. "One bloody marking on your shoulder, and all of a sudden you behave like a tart," she mumbled and stood there a moment longer before realizing she needed to do something with his body. She couldn't leave him in the field. If she wasn't going to take his life and bury him in the woods, then she had no choice but to help him – maybe back to good health and then shoving him on his way was the only other option.

Unsure of her sense of reason, Linzi decided to stop overthinking and began moving toward resolution. Her eyes drifted over to him once more, the healer in her already working through a concoction she would need to pull from the herb garden just behind the house to offer balm to the wounds on his chest, stomach, and back. It would take more than a quick remedy to fix him, and the chances of his survival might be slim. However, she refused to be the barbarian these beasts trying to take her country were.

She grabbed the kitchen knife laying still on the ground by the Saxon and then hurried back toward the house, the trickle of liquid running down her open palm giving her pause. She lifted her hand, grimacing at the pain caused by reopening the rope burn, which had yet to close from the day before. Blood dripped down her wrist and ran down a crimson line toward her white gown.

"No... damn." She slung her hand, blood decorating the ground before her. The thought of tearing a bit more off her night dressing crossed her mind, but she pushed it quickly aside. It was already too small and tight, another inch off the bottom and she would find herself not only starting to act, but also looking like a tart from the nearby town.

She shook her head and jogged toward the house, slipping into the coolness it offered. She had no time to catch her breath. She tossed the kitchen knife on the table before she checked on her father, ensuring he was still all right. Nothing but serenity greeted her, the fresh smell of honeysuckle pouring in from the door behind her and the gentle snoring of her father. She would check him again before she left the house. It seemed his fever might have dropped, his body no longer pushing heat, like the sun soon would be on the fields behind the house. It reminded her of the pressing matter outside.

She worked quickly to wrap her hand. She would need to get the large man out of the yard and bring him into the house. She had no choice. She couldn't simply deposit him in the woods and watch over him in there. What if a large animal attacked him during the night? He was much too beautiful to be given over for food. VIKING

The Saxon had to be a head taller than her and at least a hundred pounds heavier. She was strong from her years of working on the farm with her father and brother, but to think about lifting him onto a horse or dragging him back to the house from his current location was ignorant. She couldn't do it. *Impossible to do it alone.*

She stopped by her father's room again, touching his head. The wetness on his brow and hair assured what she had thought earlier. His fever had broken and though his skin was moist, at least he wasn't still so hot to the touch. He had shifted too far to the right, his lanky arm hanging off the bed, his hand slightly blue from lack of oxygen. She thought of waking him, but decided it might be easier just to pull the sheet from the opposite side of the bed, shifting him toward the middle again. She did just that, her eyes widening upon her success.

"That's it!" she whispered and hurried down the hall to Kenton's room. She ripped the sheet from his bed and stopped by the kitchen to gather a long rope. She would have to plan it just right, but if she did, the Celt would be up to the house in a matter of minutes instead of hours. She could find the strength to drag him into the house if she could just get him to the front door. Getting him in Kenton's bed would be a whole different story.

The beautiful mare she had tied up earlier stood quietly by the house, Linzi approaching the beast slowly with her hand extended once again. The horse snorted as if not wanting to be bothered, Linzi ignoring her protest as she untied her, brushed her side with her fingers and carefully put the supplies on her back. "Your master's lying near-dead in the field. I need your help with him. I know you're tired sweetie, but you'll be glad you did it. Unless he's a bastard." She moved to the front of the horse, looking into her large black eyes as she snorted again. "Is he a bastard?"

The horse pulled back a little and Linzi laughed, taking the animal's response as a sign that perhaps the Celt was a terror to the lands and all humans within them, but not to his riding companion. She walked the massive beauty back down the hill, the horse stopping and leaning over, breathing in deeply against the Saxon's hair. The locks lifted a little, his hair seemingly stiff with grime, blood, and sweat.

Linzi moved down the body of the horse, pulling the sheet off and unwrapping the Saxon's knife she now possessed. She cut two large holes in the material, not too close to the top.

"I hope this'll work. It'd be a whole lot easier if he just woke up and carried his own self to the house, but life never seems to provide a simple answer, does it?" She glanced over at the horse who simply stared absently at her. "I know you understand me. God gave you a brain and sense to do all you do. Don't look at me like that."

The animal snorted again and looked away, leaning over to pick at a small patch of grass at its feet. Linzi smiled, wishing they had more than the one horse they did own and the little lot of chickens and pigs. She wanted another horse, the last one having gone to the market when times got tough the summer before. It had almost felt like offering a good friend up to be butchered.

She let her wayward thoughts dissipate, standing and forcing herself to focus on weaving the rope into the open holds. She moved beside the inactive Saxon and laid the sheet out beside him, unsure of how to pull him onto it. She straightened and walked around him a few times, the horse making noises beside her as if trying to communicate the proper way to complete the task.

"Hush, lest you wake him." She patted the horse's snout and knelt down on the side of the man, slipping her hands under his upper back and upper thigh. She gritted her teeth and pulled with all her might, the massive muscles lining his body weighing far more than she expected. He lifted only slightly, but Linzi refused to give up and continued to pull. She fell to her knees, her feet pushing hard in the dirt behind her as he rolled over onto his chest and face, a soft grunt warning her that he wasn't far from consciousness.

"One more time," she whispered, shuffling forward a few steps and starting the process all over again. Her breathing grew labored, her hair collecting sweat as she grunted loudly and pulled, then pushed with all her might. He flipped back onto his back, a soft cough leaving his cracked lips. He was far too close to death's door for her to tarry any longer.

She stood, wiping her hands on her nightgown and looked up at the horse. "Your turn."

Connecting the ropes to the horse's saddle wasn't too difficult, but getting her to move over hill as the large Saxon rode on the makeshift pulley behind her was testing. She patted the horse's butt multiple times, popping the mare and pulling the reins. After what felt like forever, she finally had the horse tied up in the barn unseen from anyone who might come back, and the dying Viking lying on the sheet at the front entrance to the house.

She stepped over the massive man's body and walked into the darkness of the kitchen, pouring a quick drink of water and spilling it down her chin and chest. She needed to hurry. The afternoon would soon be wasted for naught and if she didn't finish planting seeds for the harvest, there would be nothing to show for it but starvation and another tombstone on the hill. Maybe two stones and another unmarked one.

She hurried to the door, bending over and lifting the top of the sheet where the Saxon's head lay. She cried out as the material bit into her wounded hand, the jolt of pain rushing from her palm up her arm. She stood on shaking legs, breathing in deeply and talking herself past it all. With a big heave, she began the momentum of pulling the stranger to her brother's room. She paused at her own door, looking down at the destroyed sheet that once belonged to Kenton. *This isn't going to work.*

The Viking would have to take her room. Kenton's room was too close to her father's and the door to the house. Plus, no way would she have him resting on an unmade bed, the mattress too scratchy and rough. She would just have to give up her room, wash the tattered sheet below him, fix it and then use it for herself.

Kenton wasn't here anyway. He wouldn't mind her sleeping in his bed... as long as he didn't know the real reason she was there. For all she knew, he might never return.

The thought created a lump in her throat that burned more than her tired muscles.

She focused again on the impending issue lying at her feet. It was better than thinking about her brother. Making a quick turn, she worked to get the Saxon into her room, his body lying lifeless on the floor below her bed. She knelt down beside him on the floor, leaning over to listen for breathing. He was alive and yet hadn't given anything more than a subtle jerk here and there since she'd dragged him from the field. She sighed softly, standing and walking to the kitchen. Her mother often used witch-hazel to wake them when they were kids. She remembered her mother using it the time Kenton had tried to fly and jumped off the barn roof. He'd landed in a large pile of hay, thankfully not breaking anything, but had bumped his head and passed out. Her mother had used the hazel then. Perhaps it would work now just as well.

Linzi grabbed the small jar of the herb and rushed silently back to the bedroom. She hesitated a moment before quickly fixing her pillow and covers to hold him. She then grabbed a towel and basin, filling it with water and walking carefully back to the room. She got on her knees and washed the Saxon's chest and face, taking care to not hurt the various scratches and cuts on his beautiful body. The designs drawn on him were vast, his skin more colored than not. It reminded her of the ink still healing on her shoulder.

She wanted to ask him a million questions but knew she never would. It didn't stop her from wondering things.

Saying a soft prayer to the heavens, she pulled out the witch-hazel and placed it before him, the male breathing it in at a steady rate. His eyes opened quickly, his body jolting him as he looked around wildly. Linzi yelped, covering her mouth, and fell back against the wall afraid her father might hear her and rush in. She should have checked him after she brought the Saxon in.

"Where'm I?" His words were slurred, his eyes growing heavy again. "Who're you?"

Linzi moved fast, reaching to pull him up before he passed out again. "Yer safe. I need to get you to the bed. On yer stomach."

He grunted, his eyes opening and closing as if exhaustion sat heavy on him. She debated about using the witch-hazel again, but he made an effort to sit. Linzi rushed to his side and slipped his arm around her shoulders. She staggered under his weight when he finally stood, letting her go and pressing his hands to the bed before him. One hand reached up and undid the front of his pants, the breeches falling to the floor around his ankles.

Linzi reached for him as he began to fall forward, helping him onto his stomach and having to reposition him one limb at a time as he passed out again. She tugged his pants from his legs and tried not to stare at the perfect curve of his rear. She grabbed the water basin and towel and finished washing him up, her heart pounding inside her chest. She avoided the areas she thought he might not appreciate much, her gratefulness of him being on his stomach almost overwhelming.

She'd never seen a man naked, but if it was anything like her more adventurous friend described, she was more than intrigued. If the Saxon's backside was this appealing, she was terrified to even imagine him the other way... but it didn't stop her from wondering.

Chapter 2

Marcus

"I don't see why that was bloody necessary. It'll take me the better part of a week for this damn wound to heal!" Marcus growled at the large man before him, the wrapping around his upper chest biting into the soft flesh under his arms. Why Marcus had even bothered to bow to Halfdan's wishes irked him. He was trained to be in charge, born to lead, and yet this oaf had once again gotten his way.

"Stop your whining! Without the proof of the large wound, there would be no clout to our lies. We need to show the men Erik wounded you—that he turned on you from insanity. It would be his word against yours." The older man reclined in a large wooden chair, his shoulders lifting in a shrug meant to demean Marcus. His tactics were always emotional because the fat arse was physically useless should a brawl be in order.

"I understand that, but I rather prided myself on my appearance before you took a damn blade to the front of my chest. I look like a fucking savage now."

Halfdan flicked his wrist as if the injury meant nothing. "Women love scars, boy. It is the mark of a real warrior. If you would stop tormenting yourself about what you think should be yours, and just enjoy all that's been laid before you, you might know that. Stop crying about not being Erik. Or his spot in the lineage. It means nothing." He scoffed. "When's the last time you've forced a tart to beg for pleasure?"

Marcus rolled his eyes and walked toward the opening of the tent, looking out as the men wandered up from various areas, all of them looking worn, their numbers running a little too thin for his liking. "I'm not having this conversation with you. We're not family, nor friends. When do we explain the situation to the men?" That's all he cared about. And the scar that would ruin his perfect skin. Unless it would make others believe he was the warrior that stopped the mad prince.

"I'll tell them." Halfdan made a dismal effort to get off his chair. He settled back down and grabbed his pewter cup of wine. "Better yet, you tell them. I don't mind lying, but oftentimes the flavor of a wicked one such as this will sit on your tongue and rot for weeks."

Marcus glanced over his shoulder, his jaw locked in place with disdain. He tried to look the part but was more than pleased to be the one to carry the news to the men. The glory would be his, not Halfdan's. "Fine. I'll tell them, but you need to be beside me as an eyewitness to the events."

Halfdan stared at Marcus as if he had the ability to read inside the young man's mind. He finally pushed himself out of his seat and gulped the last of his wine down. As he wiped his bearded chin he said, his voice low and raw, "It was your cousin in my way, Marcus. You're simply a pawn. Should I begin to feel that you're a threat, the same thing that happened to Erik can happen to you. Do not test me in this, nor should you go gathering ideas of grandeur and hopes of being King. That position is mine and mine alone." His last words would have sent a chill down the dead corpses' spines who lay on the battlefield had they heard him.

A nod was all the commander got. Marcus slipped out of the tent and walked toward a large group of men, a slight limp to his gait.

John, one of Erik's most loyal commanders, rose as Marcus approached, the older man's eyes rolling over him as he moved with feigned emphasis. "Where's Erik? Have you found him?"

Marcus held up his hand, his own leadership style quite different from that of his beloved cousin. Erik being the crowned prince of Denmark most likely made way for the immediate level of loyalty he received amongst the men. Marcus discarded the thoughts and moved into the center of the circle, purposely ignoring John's questions. "Gather the troops. Halfdan and I have an announcement. It's regarding our future plans. I'll not speak more than once on it, so leave no one out less they fall behind or meet a bloody end in their undeserved confusion."

The men stood around him, milling about as they walked through the large camp, yelling and calling all to come. The tents spread far and wide, the edge of the forest on their northern front the borderline of Scotland. The sea town behind them still burning bright, the sky littered with the smoke that billowed toward the heavens. They left nothing alive, taking what they wanted and destroying the rest. The English or Scottish that had escaped would not get far. They too would soon be left to lie on the earth forever.

The sound of soft cries caught Marcus' attention. He turned around to see a group of women huddling in front of a large tent, most of them crying. Those that had been crying hysterically had been physically warned to shut their mouth. Now their cries were more the sound of whimpering, like a beaten dog. He scoffed and turned back to the meeting spot, Halfdan walking up to his left.

Marcus puffed his chest out, wincing at the pain it caused. "Women brought from the city? Seems some of them didn't make it all the way here. Shame." His voice held no emotion, his words casual conversation with no invested backing. He said the words to himself, but just loud enough in case someone heard. "They're of no concern to me, or us. I'm not interested in bedding a woman whose desperation stinks of fear." That had never been a problem for him before, but now he held a different position and the men need not know that, or should one say otherwise, he would soon find his heart outside of his chest.

"Men. My men. I understand you more than Erik did." His words brought murmurs from the crowd of men near him. Marcus raised his voice. "These women may or may not be virgins." He chuckled. "But they will all be tarts by morn, and know their way around a man. You'll each take one tonight, or share. Whatever. I don't care." He eyed a dark haired maiden with terrified eyes that flew around the men. He would have her. He licked his lips.

Halfdan stood just behind him. "The tension on you is almost tangible. I don't want the men to see. Or question your actions."

"What I do is none—"

Halfdan moved in front of him faster than Marcus suspected the man capable. He wrapped a beefy hand around Marcus' throat, squeezing tightly. "Don't forget your place, *boy*. You might be willing to kill a prince, but you haven't the bits to stab a king. Speak to me one more time with familiarity and I shall have no use for you," he growled, releasing Marcus.

"Yes, Sire." Marcus stood, his heart pounding in his chest, hate rolling in his stomach. He rubbed his neck, trying to soothe the pain. He was beyond subservience but knew his chances of a future in the palace resided on victory in the battlefield.

"Don't misstep again."

Marcus bit his tongue to stop himself from replying. He moved to future thoughts. If he were the only one to return and Nathaniel, their King, lie dead, he would be the next heir. He could not get there without Halfdan. He nodded meekly.

"Good. Remember that."

Marcus looked over his shoulder, a thin brunette standing over to the side, her eyes removing his clothes without shyness. The terrified one no longer held his interest. This one was a whore by nature. She would soothe his disgruntled mood, or at least make the men think so. He pointed at her. "You, go to my tent and wash up." He pointed to a lad waiting for an order. "Take this one to my tent."

"Which tent is yours?" the idiot boy asked.

His face burning, Marcus hit him on the back of the head. "It's the one to the right of the commander's tent." He turned back around, the men beginning to line up. *Perfect.* His interest in sating himself in the back end of a female was null, but to shut the old coot up next to him and make himself appear more in tune with the men before him, he'd take her and be done with it.

Halfdan shot him a disgusted look. "Gather up. I haven't the time nor the desire to stand here and wait. Move quickly and save your exhaustion for your cot." Halfdan progressed to the center of the small grassy pasture, men moving to crowd in around him.

Marcus didn't have a choice but to follow. He stood behind Halfdan this time and waited until the area was covered with soldiers before stepping to the center. He turned to address the crowd of men that had not taken women. *Erik's men.* "Many of you are wondering where my cousin, Erik, is."

"You mean our crowned prince, Erik," John spoke plainly, standing on the first ring of the inner circle.

Marcus shifted to face him, pinning him with an undeviating stare. "Is he not one in the same?"

The question died between them as Halfdan moved beside Marcus, placing a hand on his shoulder and squeezing. "I think I should make this announcement. It hits far too closely to home for Marcus." He looked down at Marcus and nodded. "Remove your shirt and show them what happened."

Marcus exhaled softly, as if put off by the request, before stepping to the side and pulling the shirt from his upper body, grimacing due to the pain that truly lanced his chest. He pulled at the dressing carefully, a soft growl leaving his mouth as he released himself from it. The deep cut seeped with blood, the skin around the opening red and puffy. He would be lucky if he didn't die from an infection. Perhaps that was Halfdan's purpose all along?

"What happened, Marcus?" someone called out.

"Didn't have Erik there to protect you, old boy?" one of Erik's soldiers laughed. "Finally got a lovely scar to prove your fight for victory with the rest of us?"

"Erik isn't here anymore." Marcus kept his tone neutral, careful not to cause the wrong excitement in the men. "He went rogue. I kid you not. As he left, I caught up with him, questioning his exit. He grew angry. We fought." He paused for dramatic effect, touching the skin by his wound. "I can only assume he meant to scar me and not kill me because of us being kin."

"What he means is that Erik is not in his right mind." Halfdan stepped beside Marcus, his elbow brushing Marcus' wound. "Marcus rode across the threshold and was attacked by a small band of Scots, Erik's actions shocking and yet true." Halfdan motioned for one of the men to move toward Marcus. "Help redress the wound."

"Erik would never betray us by leaving." John stepped up, anger covering his grungy features. "Did something happen? What's the rest of the story?"

"There is no rest of the story. He wanted to play the hero. He's hated our commands since we arrived in this wretched country. He planned to defy his brother! Did you not know he believed himself better than you all?" Marcus turned full circle, staring at all of them, his voice booming across the silence of the evening as it rolled in.

"He was a prince," John argued, not believing him. "Of course he was elevated above us. We are his subjects."

"This wasn't about his royal bloodline, John. He believed that we were vulgar and demons from hell itself. He hated every one of you. I thought—I hoped—I might talk him out of walking away from us, I couldn't. I tried to stop him, to reason with him, and he cut me from shoulder to stomach. He didn't even look himself when he left, almost as if he knew death awaited him beyond the trees." Marcus touched his fingers to the bridge of his nose.

"Why didn't you go after him? Call on some of us?" another voice yelled from the middle of the crowd.

Halfdan stepped up, his expression one to remind the men he wasn't to be challenged by their common questions and simple minds. "Erik was told to ride out and scout with Marcus. They were at the northern tip and alone. It would be difficult to force Erik to do anything if one were healthy and fully strengthened, no?"

They all mumbled and grumbled their responses, agreeing with the large commander before them.

"It is what it is. Marcus tried to stop him, and for that will suffer greatly for the next few weeks. He will be moved up to take Erik's spot and will ride beside me. Not one word from any of you or I will ensure your death is slow and painful. I will not risk this campaign." Halfdan cleared his throat. "Your prince has abandoned you, but your King still sits in Denmark and as his right hand, I will continue to bring victory upon your heads. May Valhalla accept Erik in its bosom and may you fight our next battle in remembrance for who he was before the craze of battle took hold."

The men chanted loudly, Marcus pulling on his shirt and turning to walk toward his tent. There would be many questions over the next few weeks, but he would divert to Halfdan and keep his opinion regarding Erik to himself. He was the hero, the beloved one among the men. The men would love him as they once loved Erik, or still loved the bastard.

"Well, now he's rotting in a field somewhere," Marcus mumbled, walking into the darkness of his tent. He moved to light a candle, turning and looking at the life-worn woman who sat on the edge of his cot, a naughty smile on her thin lips.

"Where do you want me?" she asked, standing and pulling at her already loose dress.

"Leave it on." He motioned for her to stop. He moved to a small chair and worked to undo his breeches, dropping them to his knees. He closed his eyes and let out a long breath, weariness wrapping around him like a second skin. He sat down and leaned back, his mind taking him far from the scene before him. He didn't want a thin brunette, but a buxom redhead, her skin white as alabaster, her curves thick like a woman's should be. The ones he'd seen in the country, forbidden to them.

He motioned for the girl to come to him, his body aroused at the vision behind his eyelids. He spoke plainly, his voice without emotion, as nothing moved him toward wanting to express his heart.

"Turn around. Don't speak, don't moan, do not touch me other than to use my legs to balance yourself."

He shifted his hips up as she sat down on his lap, her warmth barely something to covet. He turned and moved his arms behind to hold the back of his head. Marcus let the moment physically be present, but emotionally somewhere a long ways away.

He could hear her taking pleasure from him, his body made for sex, his stamina exhausting at times. He reached up and wrapped his hand around the back of her neck, shifting himself to sit up straight. The other hand on her hip, he drove himself into her, the beautiful Scottish girl in his mind's eye moaning and taking him with vigor. The girl of his dreams looked over her shoulder, her eyes blue as the sea, her fiery mane wrapped around his fingers and whispered the words he needed most, "I want only you."

His head dropped back, his body convulsing over and over. When his heart stilled, he pushed the tart from his lap and stood, pulling his pants up over his hips.

She cried out in surprise as she fell to the floor.

He stepped over her. "Get out. Don't come back." He walked from the tent, his body cooling quickly, the girl in his dreams only a dying hope.

Chapter 3

Linzi

Another long afternoon of working the field alone left her bone tired, her mind having shifted from Kenton back to the Saxon lain up in her bed. Always back to the stranger in her house. With her luck, she would return home only to find him dead. A smile touched her lips at the thought of having to explain that one to her father.

"Most girls are caught kissing a boy behind the church at the edge of town, or stealing a piece of Mister McAllister's pewter jewelry, but no... you have to kill a Viking and leave him rotting in your bed. What's the matter with you girl?"

She laughed, dusting her hands on her skirt, her nightgown long gone, having been cut to shreds by her new knife. It wasn't much worth wearing anymore anyways, so using it for small towels made more sense. She wiped her brow, her long copper hair a loose bun atop her head.

The house stood quiet when she walked in, the ambiance leaving her longing for companionship. Less than a fortnight ago she, her father and Kenton had been laughing at the table, sharing something good to eat and enjoying the simplicity life had afforded them. They worked hard but were gifted with the fruits of that labor – a peaceful life in the country, away from the busyness of the small city. People being too close made her father nervous. They always wanted in your business or your pockets, or so he would remind her and Kenton all the time.

Now she had two men in the house, and neither were in any condition to speak. It was almost funny.

She stuck her head in her father's room, reaching up and pulling her hair down, letting it splay across her shoulders. Her father lay resting on his side, the water mug beside the bed on its side and empty. That was a good sign.

A muffled cough caught her attention. Linzi hurried down the hall to find the half-dead male sitting on the side of her bed, her pillow over his lap. She'd dressed his wounds, but it still left a lot of skin bare. Her cheeks warmed at the thought of him being nude under the small cotton square.

She shook her head and walked into the room. "Remind me not to lay my head on that tonight." Open mouthed, she watched the pillow as he stood, his legs wobbling underneath him.

He pulled the pillow tighter to the front of him, his eyes filled with fog and curiosity. She reached for him, catching him just before he fell and sat him back on the bed. "Where am I, woman?"

She motioned with her hand for him to lower his voice. "You're in Scotland. My name is Linzi. You'll do well to remember that. I won't go by woman. It's insulting."

He tilted his head to the side slightly, the dirt ring around his neck telling her that she'd not done as good of a job cleaning him earlier as she had thought. He stared at her, blinking continuously, as if solely focusing on her took more effort than he had. "Are all women in Scotland so crude?"

"Worse. Most of them would have slit your throat out in the field where you lay half dead. Be grateful." She moved back from him and ran her fingers through her hair, the bluest eyes she had ever seen moving up and then down as if studying her. *Checking me out, more likely.* Oddly, she didn't seem to mind.

"I guess I should feel lucky and yet, I don't." He closed his eyes, rolling his shoulders as his face grimaced with pain.

She wasn't sure what to say, as biting back at him just didn't seem fitting. She had to help him for a day or two – unless he proved to be the arse she expected he was. Then she might regret not sinking that knife into his beautiful, muscular neck. *Stop that!* she scolded herself.

"You're lucky I didn't decide to kill ya." She reached down and pulled her skirt up to mid-thigh, propping her foot on a nearby stool to untie her dusty brown boots.

He yawned and then opened his eyes. "What kind of..." He stared at her until she looked up at him and met his gaze. "Are you one of the servants here?"

She laughed, pulling the boot off her aching foot and moving to work on the other one. "You could say I'm the hired hand. I sure feel like it most days." She sat on the small stool to pull the other boot off. "Tell me your name." She'd told him hers, it only seemed fair.

"I'm hungry." He tried to sit again, his words lacking emotion altogether. She expected him to be more violent. Perhaps after a meal and regaining a bit of his strength he would prove her right.

"Tis a pleasure to meet you, *hungry*." She stood, hands on her hips. "I'm going to bathe and then I'll fix you something to eat."

"Where's your master? I need to explain my situation." He made no effort to rise, already weak from what he had tried to do. He had no strength inside him. A man as large and muscular as him, now a helpless babe.

She reached down and pulled her dress over her head, her slip small and probably inappropriate in front of the stranger, but she was hot and dirty. He would be gone soon and she could at least tell Martha she undressed in front of a sexy Viking. It wouldn't be a lie – not entirely. She'd just leave out the part that he lay half dead on her bed. Maybe she'd add that he was near naked instead. That would throw Martha off from asking any questions.

He grunted softly, his eyes moving down the front of her body. She stopped and stared at him, his fingers tightening on the pillow he held to hide his nakedness. She turned and walked to the door, reaching to open it.

His voice stopped her. "Wait. Please. Lizbeth, right? No, that's not it." His English accent sounded foreign and unique at the same time. He tried her name again. "Lins, Liz, Linzi! Linzi," he said it a second time, letting the name roll off his tongue. "I'm Erik. Please. I need to bathe as well. My wounds... I'm just not sure I can walk to the showers."

She looked over her shoulder, her hand high on the doorframe as she turned, leaning into the stretch. He was right about one thing, he wasn't fully capable of doing anything. "You were harmless when lost to pain." She was having doubts about keeping him in the house. Her father could wake any moment. The sooner the Saxon left, the better.

He tried to stand again, only to fall back on the bed with an angry grunt. "I'm rather useless, rest assured. I'll not harm you in any way. I wouldn't want your master upset with me. I simply need a place to stay for a few days to gain my strength. Then I'll be on my way."

"Look, Erik." It annoyed her he thought she was a servant. Some hired working girl. "The only master I have is in heaven, so quit referring to me like that." She huffed at him, walking over and sliding one arm around his waist, pulling his muscled arm over her shoulder. He stunk and would make the house putrid if she didn't help him bathe.

That, and seeing him naked would be a treat she couldn't even put words to.

"All you had to do was say so."

"I just did." Maybe he'd hit his head a couple times while riding injured on his horse.

"I'm aware of that, but you could have said something before getting upset with my assumptions." He helped pull himself up, his face turning pale.

She forgot her annoyance and moved closer, supporting almost all of his weight on her small frame. She wrapped a small wool blanket over his hips, keeping her eyes averted as she did so.

"Don't overdo it. I carried your sorry butt up here once. I'm not doing it again. You will sleep where you fall. I promise."

"Then I shall hope it's not in a puddle of muddy water." A smile touched his lips, followed by a soft chuckle as they started to walk toward the front of the house.

She stopped by the kitchen, carefully lowering him to the bench by the table.

"Let me get us a towel and check on my Da'. Then we can go."

He nodded, probably not understanding a word she said.

She walked quickly to the small cloth cupboard by the pantry, grabbing the last two towels. She sighed with relief that there was more than one. She hated running out of towels, which meant running through the woods naked or having to go without a bath – both horrid experiences. She had used her cut up nightgown to tend to his wounds. She would have to wash them later tonight. She stuck her finger to her lips and pointed down the hall. "I'll be right back," she whispered before moving to her father's room. She touched his chest to ensure he was still breathing and not boiling again. PILLS IN VIKING TIMES ??

One pill sat on his nightstand and his color looked much better. She thought for a moment about offering the pill to Erik but remembered the witchdoctor's words. He needed all of them himself if he were to fully recover.

She walked back into the kitchen, only to find Erik trying to get up and failing to do so. He knocked a chair over in the process. Creating a racket that could wake the dead.

She rushed beside him as he muttered an apology, the tone of his voice leaving something to be desired surrounding the truth of his words. "Me Da' doesn't know yer here." She couldn't believe he hadn't woken from the noise the stranger had managed to make. She maneuvered the two of them through the kitchen door, the light of the moon bathing them as they hobbled away from the house.

The soft babble of water from the creek just beyond the house beckoned them. "Will you make it? I can pull water from the well otherwise."

"I will. Otherwise roll me in the direction of the water." He chuckled. "I apologize for having to ask you to help me. I should think my legs will be back under me tomorrow. The wounds look good. Shall I assume you cleaned and took care of me?" He looked over at her, his head tilted down, creating shadows on his high cheekbones.

The regality of his appearance stole her breath, her body housing the strongest shudder she remembered ever feeling. "Yes," she whispered and turned her attention to the ground before them, feigning her attention to their steps. She wasn't practiced with talking with men much and though she was quite confident in her own right, this man wasn't a blacksmith's son or a baker's boy – he was a warrior. His strong arms and chest showed the signs of swinging a sword all day long.

"Thank you, Linzi." Her name sounded right on his tongue, his voice littered with the pain of trying to balance and not lean too much on her. The blanket tied around his waist tangled around his knees, the idea of a kilt apparently foreign to him, making it even more difficult to walk. He cursed as his foot caught a small bump in the grass.

Linzi leaned in front of him to keep him from falling. He grabbed ahold of her, his arms strong and tight around her neck. He closed his eyes, the long lashes he was blessed with catching her attention.

"Apologies. My damn body doesn't seem to want to cooperate. I'm most likely rotting from the inside." He inhaled and grimaced. "By the smell of me, I'm sure I am."

"No, you're not rotting." She laughed despite her weariness. "It's just blood loss. Food will help. I'm not sure how you will stand in the creek though." She moved back to his side, reaching over carefully to lay her arm around his broad waist. She didn't want to press against the wound slowly healing on his back.

"I can float in the water. If you could be so kind as to help me get down into it."

She nodded, her mind buzzing with the situation presented. Never in a million years would she have thought men as handsome as the one hanging on to her existed. Not only didn't they exist, but now she got to see him awake, fully naked and possibly be asked to help bathe him. A smiled touched her lips as they stopped at the edge of the water. She shivered, not from the cold.

"How do we want to do this?" he asked, turning toward her, his knees nearly buckling.

Linzi shifted, his arms resting on her shoulders as she held him around the waist. His chest muscles twitched, the night's wind brushing through the small alcove. She hated to get her underclothes wet in the lake, but she was not going to undress in front of him and then stand nude. It was not going happen. "Let's walk slowly down into the water together. The bank drops sharply at one point. You'll have to pull the blanket off you as it's the only one we have for your bed tonight."

"You're letting me stay in the house?"

"Of course. You can take my bed and I'll take Kenton's."

"Who's Kenton?" His voice rose with jealous suspicion.

It nearly made her smile, until she thought of her brother and the possibility of the man before her taking her brother's life with his sword.

"Is he at war?" he asked when she didn't answer.

"Aren't we all?" She snorted. "Thanks to your people." He could find his own way in the creek, fall in for all she cared. She turned from him, repositioning, and took a step toward the water's edge. She felt the slight tug on the inside of her elbow. Why she paused, she did not know.

Erik did not say anything. He just slipped his arm through hers and shuffled slowly, a step behind her. He paused a moment as the blanket slipped from his hips.

Linzi, still a step in front of him, lifted her eyes skyward as she dropped the towels on the ground. She scolded herself for being so silly. She'd seen him lying naked on her bed and bathed his body when she'd brought him in. However, she couldn't stop her eyes from traveling where they wanted to. She lifted the hem of her slip as they stepped into the water. She let it fall, realizing it would be no help up against her thighs. The warm liquid slipped up over her calves, thighs and hips before she turned toward him.

Erik slipped down into the water and let only his head hover above it, his massive arms moving subtly to keep him afloat. "The bank did drop quickly. Thank you for the warning." He let the liquid splash against his face before bringing his head up again. "The water is warm. Feels so good against my skin."

She nodded, looking toward the shore. "I forgot the soap by the towels. Are you going to be okay if I get it?"

"I'm good," he muttered, turning away from her. Linzi moved back up to the shore, reaching for the soap and double-checking to be sure he was still turned before pulling her under clothes over her head. She covered her breasts and walked back toward him quickly, grateful for the coverage of the water.

He turned when the water rippled against him as she neared.

She slipped under the surface, pushing up and enjoying the moment. Her feet touched the sandy bottom. She wiped her hands on the soap and gave it to him before scrubbing her fingers in her hair.

He took it and carefully rubbed his hands together, his face lost in the shadows. She ignored him and enjoyed the soft scrub of her fingers on her scalp, the wind had blown dust and dirt into her hair and now it felt ridiculously good to have it clean.

A soft growl grabbed her attention. "What it is?" She moved toward him, leaving a comfortable distance between them.

"I can't get my left arm up to wash my hair. I swear I'm going to gut the bastard that did this to me."

She moved behind him in the water, taking the soap and letting out a soft breath, her stomach in knots. "Go under briefly and get it wet. I'll hold you to make sure you come back up."

"Is Kenton your husband?" He looked over his shoulder when she laughed sardonically.

"My brother. I should drown you for that."

Chapter 4

Erik

He didn't have time to respond, the beautiful girl behind him wrapping him in a tight hug before dragging him under the water with her. He relaxed against her, the soft press of her breasts causing him to moan under the water's reprieve. She pulled him up, Erik beyond frustrated with his sudden handicap. The water made him feel weightless until he tried to stand.

If his legs didn't work in the morning, he would lose his mind. For tonight, he would just press the thoughts away that drove him toward madness. He should simply try to enjoy the comfort of this beautiful woman who had every right to kill him, and yet hadn't.

He moved his arms, turning to look at her, the long silky strands of her red hair dancing on the top of the water's edge, begging for his fingers to touch them. Her eyes were filled with innocence, her demeanor tough only because she seemed to be alone with no one but apparently a sick father to care for her. He had gathered that much from the way she hurried to the man's room earlier. His heart ached at her plight, but his emotions lay deep before his facade of indifference. "So your brother went to fight the horrible Saxons, and what of your father? Is he elderly?"

A smile touched her mouth, the tilt of her head telling him quickly that she wasn't going to be easy to get along with. She was clever, probably very smart. He almost enjoyed the challenge she would present more than the way his body reacted to the feminine curves of her near perfect figure. She might be treated as a girl in a home of two men, but she was well into maturity, the perfect slope of her breasts and hips leaving everything to be desired. If he wasn't so weak...

"Turn around. Let's get this bath over with. I need to get back to my father. It's already late. The morning will come calling soon and I need some rest myself before it does. Two sick men and the fields to tend to, the animals and, of course, the house, and food."

He nodded and turned, the desire to look over his shoulder at her overriding the pain that laced his chest as his arms moved. He would have to think through what happened before the world dimmed, but for now, he would leave it be. It had been far too long since he felt the touch of a woman in any capacity. He wanted to revel in it under the false pretense of being weak and tired. He would leave tomorrow, but for tonight... he would simply be a man without responsibility. He wondered how she managed. She worked hard, he could see that from the subtle curve in the muscles in her arms and legs, but she also had this incredible femininity about her. He felt himself grow hard underneath the water and tried to force his thoughts away. She might not appreciate the effect she had on him. He grinned at the night sky. He was only a man. What else would be expected; in the water, under the moonlight with a naked goddess of fire-red hair offering to wash him?

Her fingernails brushed over his short hair, the tingles rushing from her touch down his neck and shoulders, his teeth clamping together to keep his groan on his tongue.

"What happened to cause you to be lying half dead in my field? Did you upset my brother?"

He could hear the teasing in her voice, trying to make her question light. He closed his eyes, his fingers itching to reach back and pull her flush against him again, to touch the silky wet skin of her leg or the curve of her backside. "Someone shot two arrows into my chest. I must have blacked out. I do remember coming to long enough to remove them, but that's all." He turned his head to the side, Linzi running her short nails down the side of his neck and moving with him as he bid her due.

"I find it hard to believe you were unable to stop them." She cleared her throat, apparently embarrassed she was referring to his strength. "Why didn't the men that meant to kill you, finish you off? No Englishman or Scot would leave you half dead, especially on the land of a simple farmer. We protect one another." *How did you escape?* The unspoken question hung in the air.

"It wasn't the enemy, but a friend." He captured her wrist with his hand, turning to face her and putting it on his cheek. "Wash my face for me." He closed his eyes, the soft panting of her breath so close, almost driving him mad. He didn't want to talk of betrayal. It hurt more than his wounds.

How long had it been since he'd made love to a woman? The better part of a year at least. He hoped tonight would break the cursed spell, but he'd not force himself on anyone. He let his hands slip into the water, brushing by his wound and flinching.

She moved away from him, her breath catching from what he could hear.

He kept his eyes shut tightly, the soap on his face thick and heavy.

"Did I hurt you?" she whispered.

"No, tis the wounds on my stomach. Just a bit more sensitive than I thought." He relaxed as she moved toward him, the water splashing against his chest. She finished washing his face and he dunked his head under the water to rinse the soap free. He set his feet on the sand and pebbles below and straightened slowly so the water could carry his lower weight without tiring him. The water came up to just above his navel. He reached up to wipe the remaining water off his face, blinking a few times to clear his vision.

She stood before him, the water lapping gently across the top of her breasts, the perfect fullness of her mouth drawing his attention. He realized what he was doing as her fists pressed against his chest, his hand behind her back as he drew her in.

"Erik! What are you doing?"

"I want to kiss you."

"W-Why?"

He laughed, the sound easing out of his tattered soul, the world looking very different on the other side of treachery. "Because you're beautiful, and all I've seen is dead and hate for three years. I apologize in advance." He brushed his lips ever so lightly against hers and then quickly released her and moved back. He lowered his body into the water and lay on his back, looking up at the moon and stars, letting the peace the gods offered him give him a rest. "Wash up and we'll head back. You need to sleep. I promise to behave properly." He sighed, refusing to glance her way as much as his body begged him to. "I shall be out of your hair tomorrow."

She didn't reply but busied herself moving her hands about her body, his mind crowded with the various places she touched, his chest burning with desire, his stomach tight with need. Food. He needed sustenance to fill his belly, it would help, and then he would sleep off the need to lose himself within her. She had saved his life. She deserved the respect of the prince within him, not the taking of the Viking he had become.

"I'm done." Her voice floated over him like the lapping of the water teasing his body.

"Good," he said, rougher than he meant to. "I may need help walking back. My feet feel grounded, but it is the water helping me more than I care to admit."

She moved toward him, reaching under his arm and pulling him toward the shore with her. It took more effort keeping his eyes averted to the tree line beyond them than physically moving. The desire to look at her scorched him inside and out. She reached for one of the towels, wrapping it around herself as he held lightly onto her shoulder, his legs gaining strength as he suspected.

Erik took the other towel from her hands, working it around his waist and turning toward her as she moved back from him, a smile on her beautiful face.

"You're standing. Stronger already." She turned and picked the blanket and her slip off the ground.

When she straightened, he reached out his finger, brushing by the strand of roses that rolled over her shoulder and disappeared into her towel, her breast surely covered by the design. His eyes moved from it to her, the moonlight allowing him the pleasure of seeing her clearly.

"This design is beautiful. It's fitting for you. Feminine and yet, fearless. I didn't know the English liked ink markings."

"I'm Scottish." She laughed softly, moving to help him once again. She left the small towel and soap by the water, her long wet hair tickling his arms as they moved.

He wasn't sure he needed the help, but her closeness was welcomed regardless.

She spoke quietly as they began to walk. "How do you know I'm fearless? We just met."

"You're not afraid to speak your mind."

She giggled, the soft shaking of her shoulders under his arm pleasant against his skin. "Just because I'm a bit mouthy doesn't mean I have courage to boot."

"I beg to differ. You walked into your fields by yours a couple of days ago and saved a Viking, moving him from the outdoors to the comfort of your bed." A thought came to him. "How did you get me into your house? I have to be three times your size."

"Twice my size and you don't want to know." She waved her hand, showing a cut that had scabbing over it. "You owe your horse a debt of gratitude."

He could hear the humor in her voice, the sound of it swelling his heart. He had wanted a woman in his life and a large field like this to work for far too many years to let the fantasy pass him by. Could he not pretend for a night like he'd finally been awarded with it all? "I shall make sure to thank her in the morning then."

She laughed again, stopping just outside the door to the house. She lowered her voice. "My father fell ill just after Kenton left. He's not elderly, but still strong and willful. He's sick with the fever, but should be back to himself soon than naught. If he hears you in the house..."

Erik nodded. "Understood."

They moved in, Linzi helping him to the large wooden table that someone had spent many long hours carving and perfecting. The wood was smooth and oiled, the touch of human hands having brushed across it enough times to leave it perfect.

"Stay here," she commanded and when he caught her hand she turned back to him. "I need clothes. I'm not serving food like this. I'll grab you breeches from Kenton, but I'm not sure they'll fit. I can wash yours in the morning, I'm not going to do it tonight."

"No. You're probably right, they won't fit. I never sleep clothed, unless I'm on the battlefield. I'd rather my wounds breathe for now."

"Suit yourself." She walked off, the towel puckered out where the curve of her rear pushed at the thin fabric. He sucked his bottom lip in his mouth, his hand pressing down on his crotch to still his thoughts and their wayward reactions. She was beyond beautiful, angelic and yet fiery. Were all Scottish women the same? If so, he had been looking at the wrong countryside for sure.

He slid his hands onto the table, stretching and turning his torso to see if he could feel the burn of healing within his chest and stomach. The loud growl of hunger caused him to tense up, the last meal he remembered eating had to be at least a few days back.

"How long was I in your field, do you know?" he called after Linzi, the lovely – what did the Scotts call their ladies again? *Lass.* The lovely *lass* walking back into the kitchen and hushing him with her motions. Her arms waved in the air, the bounce of her breasts catching his eye. He swallowed hard and turned back to admire the table.

"Da' will hear you. Keep it down."

"I forgot." He wasn't used to being commanded by a woman. He rather liked it. "How long was I out there?"

"I don't know. I brought you in the same day I found you." She moved away, the candlelight catching a glow behind her as she worked. She wore nothing beneath the long cotton dress, her level of comfort mistakenly hidden in the dress's ability to cover her. He could see every curve and muscle as she worked to make them something to eat. He swallowed hard, pressing his fingers to his eyes as he tried to think about the last moment he remembered with his men.

He didn't want to encounter tragedy, but anything might be better than unsated lust mixed with a hunger for food. He wasn't sure he could tell the difference between the two anymore. The need within him left him almost dizzy, and feeling a lack of control almost pushing him toward her and the small loaf of bread she cut. He looked over at her as she glanced at him, her finger slipping into her mouth as she licked at what had to be honey from what he could tell. He groaned, his body reacting violently to the girl.

"I'm hurrying. I'm sorry." She moved faster, grabbing two plates and set them down between them. She bowed her head and prayed quickly, Erik's eyes moving over the bread and meat, cheese, and honey.

He waited until she offered him a small plate, reaching to take a piece of everything and working hard not to swallow it whole. "Thank you." He ate fast, a sense of doom sitting upon him as if he might perish from lack of sustenance if he didn't eat faster.

She took small bites, the thickness of her hair framing her pixie-like features, giving off a purity he wanted to taste more than the honey on his tongue. "What are you thinking about? Your hunger?" Her innocent words taunted him more than she realized.

"Yes," he barked out, not meaning to sound so harsh.

"There's a little more in the cupboard. I'll get it once you finish. It might be a good idea to slow down. If you haven't eaten in a few days, your stomach might disagree and it would be a shame to waste the meal." She pushed her half eaten plate toward him. "I can go into town tomorrow after you leave, for more, so eat your fill."

"It's not the food I hunger for, Linzi." He stared at her lips, her kindness and innocence undoing him. "It's you."

Chapter 5

Linzi

She blinked, unsure of how to respond. One moment he was a gentleman, the next, a brutish Viking. She stared at her plate and then just brushed off his comments as if he hadn't spoken sensual words toward her. Standing, she picked up her plate, deposited the rest of the food on his and then smiled before walking toward the counter of the kitchen. The stark pain in her breast and stabbing need between her legs left her dizzy and confused.

It took a moment to collect herself as she held her back to him. "I'm going to go prepare the bed for you. Eat as much as you like." She turned, the look on his handsome face telling her quickly that he wasn't pleased with her lack of response to his advancement. He was looking for someone to lie with for a night and leave forever. Martha might be fine with simply having sex, but her mother had spent enough time with her when she was a young girl, explaining the importance of saving herself for the man she would spend forever with. As much as her body wanted this handsome stranger, she would not give in to the lust.

Love is a beautiful thing, and sex is all part of that, but when you give away your body, your heart goes with it, Linzi. Guard your heart along with your innocence until your prince comes, for he will be with you forever and to him, you belong entirely.

Quite sure her mother would not approve of pretending a wounded Viking soldier was her prince for a night to experience the touch of a man. She had already marked her body with ink. If she gave the wickedly delicious man in the other room her body, what guilt would that bring upon her? She had done enough foolishness the past few days to last a lifetime.

She pulled the last sheet from the small closet in her room and made the bed. Her night's sleep promised to be cold as she would leave him with the sheet and blanket so he wouldn't catch his death. That would remind her of her foolishness.

"Linzi, I will take your brother's room. You don't need to give up your bed."

She looked over her shoulder, his towel tight around his waist, his abdomen muscles chiseled into the tanned skin of his torso. His wounds blending in with the ink covering his body.

"There's only one sheet left, and I'd rather you have it. You'll be staying a week if you catch the fever." She swallowed and begged her eyes to stop roaming over his body. "Let's make sure you're well and on your way tomorrow."

He walked in, stopping behind her as she hesitated, not quite sure of his intentions. She heard of men taking women against their will, but something deep in her gut told her he wasn't that kind of man, Saxon or not.

"I'm not taking your bed from you. How will you keep warm?"

"I'll find something. I'm fine. I'm healthy. You and Da' are the sickly ones."

He reached out and touched a strand of her hair, curling it around his finger. "The blanket isn't going to offer much warmth and it's already cold in here. Let's stay together in your bed and our body heat will keep us comfortable."

She wanted to slap him. "I'm not a tart from the city, Erik!" Her hands pressed into fists against her hips. "I'll not offer my body to you for your pleasure just because you yearn for the touch of a woman. That's your problem, Saxon." Angered, she blurted out, "I'll save my innocence for the one who deserves it."

Erik pulled her close to him, his arms moving around her waist and drawing her against him, the nightgown too thin to matter as he pressed himself against her. He moved her hair and pressed his face into the side of her neck, his arms tight and chest aching in protest.

She froze, terrified she had angered him and he would toss her onto the bed and have his way. Part of her didn't seem to mind the thought.

"Save your innocence for someone who deserves such a precious gift." He moved his head to look her in the eye. "Feel the heat between us? It's created when I press tightly against you? I'm a man, so my body might betray my intentions, but I promise you, I mean you no harm. Stay warm with me, it's all I can offer you. I have nothing else. Tomorrow I leave, and you shall regain your bed and the covers that belong upon it."

Linzi was shocked by her reaction to the firm press of his body against hers, melting her resolve to withhold anything. Her mind swam, her own arms wrapping around his thick neck as the room heated all around her. Passion or lust caused such a reaction. Either way, she hated herself for enjoying it. She didn't believe after he left she would ever be able to simply sleep in this bed again.

He moved back, looking down at her, his arms dropping to his side. "Can I ask you to treat my wounds once more with whatever you've been using? It seems to be working."

She mumbled something incoherent, her cheeks burning and body hurting in ways she had never experienced before. Love created butterflies swimming in your stomach, but lust left you gasping for air, drowning under the torrential waves of desire turned to need.

She went to the windowsill and grabbed the herbs and a glass of water. "Sit," she commanded. He did as she asked. She worked the ointment onto his back, covering it with a piece of her cut nightgown before telling him to lie on his back. She rubbed the concoction onto his chest and stomach, trying not to marvel on the tight skin and ripped muscles underneath it. He stood and she quickly slid to the far side of the bed, leaving him room. "You try anything on me and I'll rip open one of those wounds and then drag your arse back out in the yard for the birds to eat." Her threat was solid, her voice far too soft and sensual.

A smile played on his lips as she huffed at him and rolled on her side, her back turned to him. He extinguished the light in the room, the small bed moving as he climbed in.

She could tell it hurt him to move as he lay down. He lay still a moment before quietly saying, "I'm going to hold you until you tell me to move away. The cold will be trapped out of the blanket, but our body heat should stay close by."

She didn't respond, her body stiffening as he moved close, his body molding around hers. He slid his arm under her neck, Linzi lifting slightly to give him room. The press of his chest against her back was nothing compared to his arousal pressed to her rear. She closed her eyes, biting her lips to keep from making a noise. The sound of her heart beating reached her ears, her breathing loud and off kilter.

"Are you comfortable?" he whispered against her neck, his other hand coming up to rest on her thigh, the nightgown having ridden up slightly.

"Yes," she whispered, hating that she had put herself in this ridiculous situation. She should have left him in the fields. Stupid Saxon. VIKING

"You're a terrible liar. Just relax against me. I'm not going to hurt you or do anything more than what I'm doing. Feel the cold on our faces?"

"I feel it," she lied. All she felt was the heat from her body begging to be tampered with.

"And the warmth at your back?" He picked his hand up from her thigh, moving his chest from her and rubbing firm circles into the muscles of her back.

She rolled her shoulders in, her body so tense from working so hard and now from the sensual press of his body to hers. "I'm grateful for the warmth."

"You've been working that field out there by yourself?" He continued to rub her back, his crotch still tucked tightly against her rear, his sex jerking from time to time.

She wondered if he were doing that on his own or if his anatomy just caused it to happen. Martha always made fun of boys and their inability to not get a hard-on. The joke was that they were dense as could be and would hump a tree because their blood was in their pants and their brained suffered from lack of oxygen. She smiled in the dark, her pulse ticking in her throat and wrist hard enough that it was noticeable to her.

"Linzi? Did you fall asleep?" He moved his hand back to her leg, his strong fingers sliding down the outside of her thigh before splaying his fingers to touch her skin. His chest pressed against her back, his lips brushing past her ear as he spoke.

She moaned softly, unable to help herself. She pretended to cough, her pathetic means of trying to cover up her desire. "I'm not asleep." She inhaled and let a slow breath out. "I have to work the field alone right now, but it's okay. My mother did the same when she was alive and Kenton and I were too young to help. Father had gone to help fight in the last war and we had to keep things up here." She stiffened again, Erik's fingers moving on her thigh in soft circles. He moved around her leg, never moving up higher than she felt comfortable with.

"Your turn," he whispered as chill bumps broke out against her skin.

"You want me to rub your back?" She started to move and he stilled her with his arm wrapping around her, his fingers reaching out to hold her just below her breasts on her stomach. She held her breath until he answered, his words softening her a little.

"No, you can ask me a question if you like."

"Oh." She should be tired, but everything inside her seemed so awake at the moment. She relaxed against him. "What did you mean when you said you were injured by a friend, not an enemy?"

"The arrows came from my side." Erik sighed as if physically feeling the blow of betrayal. "I'll have to go back and face who deceived me. Someone I once called friend."

"Do you know who did it?" She turned in his arms, wanting to see his face. The heavy emotion that sat in his voice left her heart aching in her chest.

It was a mistake to face him; the thickness of his arm muscles and sensual curve of his lips left her stomach fluttering, her resolve turning to mush. If he but whispered her name, her innocence would be damned.

"I don't. I can only imagine one man wanting me dead. Our commander, Halfdan." He shook his head as if a foggy memory was trying to take hold. "Or Marcus."

"Who's Marcus?" she whispered.

"My cousin."

She stared at the outline of his handsome face. "Someone in your own family would mean to have you killed?"

"It wasn't Marcus. He came to help me..." He sighed softly, his strong fingers brushing her hair from her face. "None of this is your concern. Sleep now. Let's find comfort amidst the warmth of our bodies tonight."

She nodded, reaching up to brush her finger along his face before feeling the pull of sleep finally tugging her down. *"I've never seen a more beautiful monster than you, Erik."* She thought she had said the words in her head.

He laughed, the sound jolting her awake slightly. "Am I a monster?"

Clearly she hadn't. "You're a Saxon. Straight from the belly of hell. I cannot imagine why your King would send his people to kill and destroy." She yawned softly, tucking her head and pressing her cheek to his chest as she snuggled in closer. He tightened his arms around her and kissed the top of her head. Linzi knew she could easily fall in love with the feeling of being trapped against him.

Erik lie quiet a moment before sharing his thoughts out loud. "Power corrupts, I suppose. The King and, actually, his father before him have their reasons for doing what they do."

"I hope the whole family burns in hell. They deserve it for all they've taken. May they never find peace, nor rest, nor love, even after they die." She huffed loudly.

Erik moved his legs to wrap around hers. He chuckled quietly. "I think your desires have been heard by the gods already, beautiful girl. They suffer more than you imagine."

"Good," she whispered, removing the last inch of space between them as she slipped into lustful dreams.

Sometime in the middle of the night Linzi woke, her hair matted with sweat, her skin sticky and uncomfortable. She pulled from Erik's grasp, sitting up and fanning herself. He moved to sit up beside her, pulling her hair from her back and holding it up as he blew cold air on her.

"I think your plan to keep warm worked far too well."

"My attraction to you knows no bounds, I think." He laughed and gingerly lay back down before reaching up to pull her on top of his chest. She lay with her hips on the bed tucked close beside him, and her breasts pressed against his chest as her hair pooled around them.

He bit his lower lip as he stared at her. "Kiss me, Linzi. I beg you. Just one kiss. Let me taste your sweetness for a moment before we part ways tomorrow and I never see you again. You'll be the one to haunt my dreams for the rest of my life, I promise you that."

She was sure he would covet her dreams as well. She leaned in, his fingers tightening in her hair as he moved up like a viper, his mouth warm and wet, the soft groan from his need spilling onto her tongue. She opened her mouth, her fingers pressing into the soft flesh of his chest as he took advantage of her offering. His tongue pressed against hers, rolling softly against her own as his other hand slid down her back, running over her nightgown and grasping her backside.

A tremble rolled down her spine, her own moan rumbling into his mouth. Untasted desire had her moving from the bed to climb onto his body to open herself fully up to his needs.

The sound of her father calling her name threw cold water on the moment, the kiss broken and her bolting from the bed to attend to him.

She heard Erik sigh in disappointment as her heart pounded and breasts ached. She lifted a small prayer of thanks to the heavens as she raced to her father.

Erik had to leave in the morning or she would be lost to him. Plain and simple.

Chapter 6

Erik

The heat in the room is what finally woke him, his body sticking to the sheets, his lips parched. Erik sat up slowly, pulling the softened cotton covering from his chest and looking down the length of his body to assess his wounds. He touched the soft sore, the small cotton dressing Linzi had affixed to him seemed to be holding up well considering the heat. That girl was fire and water.

He stood from the bed, stretching and listening for the sound of her moving somewhere in the house. Nothing. Wrapping the sheet around his waist he walked toward the second to last door in the small hallway, her brother's room dark and cool. Grabbing a pair of breeches, he slipped them on. They fit tightly but would do. Erik pulled a blue shirt over his head and walked through the quietness of the small home.

She had never come back to bed the night before, his hopes of making love to her before leaving seemed nothing more than a dream. Disappointment turned into anger as his thoughts shifted from the beautiful lass to the betrayal that rode him hard. How someone would go against him was hard to fathom, but with the right weapons anything might be possible. Out of habit, he touched his hips, knowing he would find nothing and yet unable to help himself.

His knife.

"Where is the damn thing?" he grumbled. He must have dropped it when he lost consciousness. He had no sword or the previous knife his mother had carved for him. He walked out of the house, his eyes scanning the horizon for Linzi. Her fiery hair caught his attention, long strands of it billowing behind her as she bent over in the field, her body lithe and resilient. A cry of frustration lifted from her, the shovel in her hands beating at the ground beneath her with no avail. He turned and walked back into the house, getting his shoes and moving back out to help her. He thought of checking on her father but decided against it. He would be gone before the man ever knew he had even been there.

She looked up as he approached, her brow relaxing and a smile sliding across her beautiful mouth. His heart shuddered at the loss of what might have been if he wasn't on the hunt for his assassins. He could have stayed with her, made her his, and taken care of her father's land alongside her. Again dreams lost to the wind.

"Hi, sleepy." She winked and bent over, the soft white shirt she wore tucked into her black skirt, the material fitting and accentuating all of the places he desired to touch. "I didn't realize Saxons needed so much beauty sleep."

"You should have woken me. I could have helped."

She looked up again, smirking as she extended the shovel toward him. "Be my guest."

He took it and laughed, unable to remain stoic around her. His lack of care and hard demeanor had always been the core of his being, the center of his structure. To relax before her and just be was a breath of fresh air. His body felt strong and nearly healed.

He glanced down at the handle as she moved to pick up a small jug of water, the front of her shirt opening just enough for his eyes to catch a glimpse of her luscious skin.

"Why is there blood on the handle?"

She held up her petite hand, the wrapping on it soaked in blood. Concern laced him as he dropped the tool and took her wrist, working to unwrap it carefully.

"What did you do?" he asked, dropping the cloth to the ground beside him. The cut was angry and messy with the first signs of infection. He had seen it last night in the creek but hadn't paid proper attention to it. *Too lost in the rest of her body*, he scolded himself.

"Kenton left and Da' was ill, so I taught myself to fight the other day."

"And you fought how? I've never killed a man with the palm of my hand." He smiled, unable to help himself.

"I got a rope burn lifting the bag of sand I pulled up into a tree. I pretended it was an attacker."

He turned her hand over, surprised he hadn't noticed how busted up her knuckles were. He reached for her other hand, pulling her carefully toward the house with him. "Let me patch you up properly. You'll do no one any good losing that hand. You need to stop using it, Linzi."

She scoffed. "There isn't exactly a lot of help around here. I figure I have a day or two before the rains move in. The seed from last harvest has to be planted or we'll starve to death. That field is our only means of supporting ourselves in this war ranging nearly in our backyard."

He looked over his shoulder as they walked, his heart beating faster than it did in the midst of a battle. Was this girl stealing his heart? Was it possible or was he simply beaten down from all he had been through over the last few years and was now looking for a reason to feel something—anything? "You can't use that hand. It is my turn to help you. I'll stay another day and work the field." *Just feed me and let me sleep against you once more and then I'll go.* He didn't wait for a response but walked into the house, Linzi just behind him. He pulled open cabinets until he located supplies to patch her up.

Working quickly as she stared at him with her mouth slightly open, Erik cleaned her hand and pressed ointment to the wound before wrapping it again. "No more using this today. It needs two days to heal. I work fast and I'm strong again. I can take care of the field."

"No." She finally spoke. "You could barely walk yesterday. You aren't healed yet. I can do it. I'll just wrap an extra—"

He cut her off, stepping close to her and tilting her chin up with his finger. His breath caught in his chest, his body hardening at the innocent beauty that sat on the girl before him. She was a treasure and deserved to be treated as one. The thought of another man treating her as anything caused him to growl softly.

She pulled back, rolling her eyes at him. "If you're going to get testy about it, then fine, do it yourself. If you pass out, don't you dare expect me to drag you back up here! You've been warned." She shrugged and walked out of the house, the sway of her hips drawing his attention.

He followed her. "Did you drag me yesterday? How uncouth." He laughed as she glared at him with warning to watch himself.

"You're lucky I did anything."

"Damn right I am. I'm incredibly thankful." He stretched his arms toward the sky, eager to test the return of his strength. "I would have killed and taken my... hey, speaking of, have you seen my knife? It's small, with carved detail on the handle and script on the blade. Saxon writing." They stopped by the field, Erik leaned over to grab the shovel before she did, trying to pin her with a stern gaze and knowing he failed miserably.

"And if I did see it?" She pressed her good hand to her hip and tilted her head, red locks spilling down her chest and almost touching her belt line.

"I want it back." He lifted the shovel and drove it into the ground, his body screaming in protest. He swallowed the pain and continued to tear up the earth before them as he spoke to her.

"What if I want to keep it as payment..." Her lips pressed together as she thought. "For saving your life?"

He tried not to smile and keep his face serious. He was quite sure he would give her anything she desired. "I guess that might be fair. I'd have paid you with something quite important to me, so the knife would be fitting. You like it?" He looked down, trying not to focus on her lest he cut the edge of his toes off with his aim.

"Why is it so important to you?" Linzi asked hesitantly. She leaned over and picked up the small canteen, opening it and offering it to him when he stopped for a moment. She took the jug and lifted it to his lips, careful not to let any of the precious liquid drip on his chin wasted. He wiped his mouth with the back of his hand and began working once more.

"It was the last gift my father gave me before he passed. My mother worked to carve the design in it. My name is engraved on the handle as well if you look closely." He shrugged and grunted loudly as his shovel hit a large rock. "I hoped to give it to my son one day." He waved his hand. "It doesn't matter."

"You want children?" she whispered, the change in her tone giving him pause.

He smiled as she put the canteen down and crossed her arms over her heart as if hoping to protect herself from whatever had begun between them. "Yes, and a wife." He looked around the large grassy field in front of them and turned to admire the forest behind them before looking back to her. "And a beautiful plot of land like this one." He hit the ground hard with the shovel, dirt flying in the process. "Alas, life has laid other plans for me... but one day."

"If the knife is a family heirloom, I don't want it." Linzi glanced toward the top of the hill, where gravestones sat amidst the grass.

Erik continued to dig at the ground but averted his eyes to watch her, wondering what she might be thinking.

"My mother gave me a necklace I'd sooner die than part with. I didn't realize the significance with the blade." She took a few steps back and sat down, tucking her long shapely legs under her as she stared at her injured hand.

"Keep it. I'm sure if you sold it in the nearby village, it would bring you and your father enough funds to help you through a year." It hurt him to talk as if the thing held no significance, but he found himself suddenly willing to do anything for this woman. "The small gem near the handle is real, from the mines in Syria."

"Who are you, Erik? Are you a slave of the Celt's, or were you born to be one of their soldiers?" She shook her head.

He stopped, wiping his brow as a means of delaying his response. To tell her he was the crowned prince might embarrass her for her nasty remarks toward the royal family, or anger her that he was birthed from the *demons* as she had put it. He would be leaving her soon and so would his white lie. "I am nothing more than a Saxon man's son, a soldier to the cause simply because I was forced to fight. I'd rather be a farmer or a rancher of sorts, anything that would bring a peaceful life instead of the one I've been given." He ignored the fire in his belly, the whisper of reason to come clean with the lass and just be truthful to her.

"Where will you go from here? When you leave? Will you be forced to fight us again? To come here and take my land?"

He looked up at her as the sun pressed against him, his legs beginning to give way to occasional tremors. He dropped the shovel and walked toward her, reaching for her hand. She granted him the prize as he pulled her to her feet and released her, pointing to the house. "I need to rest and then I'll get back to it."

"Are you not going to answer my questions?" Her face showed the fear of what she believed his answer to be.

He had no idea what he would do. Only that he would hunt down and kill those who had gone against his brother, the king. "I am, but first you answer mine."

"Not this again." She huffed softly.

Erik reached over and wrapped his arm around her small shoulders, pulling her to his side as they walked the short distance to the house. "Why didn't you come back to me last night?"

She stopped, pulling from him as her face hardened. "I had to help my father."

"I'll agree he was the reason you left me aching and in need of you. But why didn't you return?"

She diverted her eyes, her fingers reaching up to pick the soft skin from her bottom lip. "I guess I was... I don't know..." She hesitated and stared at the dirt beneath their feet. "I was scared."

He closed the small gap between them, his hands sliding along her jawline, fingers slipping into the long strands of her hair as he held her still. "I wouldn't hurt you, lass."

She stared at him defiantly. "You wouldn't mean to hurt me, but you would."

Her brazen words sent his heart racing. "I know you're a virgin, Linzi. I'd have been careful with your gift. I know you want to save it. There are other things—"

"It's not my body I'm worried about, Saxon. It's my heart."

Chapter 7

Linzi

Anticipation swam in her belly, the blue-eyed Viking before her holding on tightly to her face, his hungry gaze brushing from her lips to her eyes. He was going to kiss her and if he didn't, she would do it herself. He needed to have left earlier that morning, her resolve to move past the desire that burned inside of her falling by the wayside.

He leaned in, his tongue brushing his lips before he pressed them to hers. She slipped her arms around his waist, her fingers working up the back of his shirt to feel the warm moist skin of his back. Smooth as silk and stretched across thick muscles, she groaned at the desire to see him naked and lain out on her bed again.

He moved one hand from her face, wrapping it around her and pressed against her lower back until no space existed between them. She lifted to her toes, licking at his mouth with a passion she hadn't known capable of existing. He pulled back only long enough to scorch her with his gaze. He tucked his head against the side of her neck and moved his hand over her rear, grabbing the back of her thighs and lifting.

A small sound of surprise lifted from her as he pulled her legs around his thick waist, his teeth brushing by the base of her neck. Linzi released herself to the moment, her eyes closing and head falling back as a heavy sigh left her. This was right – so purely simple. The need to be pressed to the ground by his desire, to feel him sating himself against her as she offered all she was to his release. She didn't need to save her innocence for anyone else. It had been him she'd been saving it for.

He walked them toward the house, pressing her to the outside wall of the structure and grinding against her, his grunts hoarse and needy. She ran her fingers through his hair, the sensation of his carnality undoing her from the inside out. "I want to be inside of you, Linzi. I want to see the pleasure on your face when I bring you to the edge of release and throw you over the cliff." He kissed her neck again, his lips so soft, tongue so wet.

She didn't know how to respond, so she didn't, the soft whimper of her own need escaping her mouth when he looked up, his fingers digging into the softness of her rear.

He kissed her softly, his fingers brushing against the most intimate part of her. She yelped softly, never having experienced something so divine. It was wrong and her father would kill her, but nothing would replace the feeling of Erik pressed against her, his words wicked, his movements controlled and sensual.

He broke the kiss, lifting her a little more as he brushed the tip of his nose against her breast, her arousal causing her nipple to bud. She looked down, air seemingly so difficult to find as she watched the enjoyment on his features as he placed his mouth on the small pebble that pressed against her shirt, his groan breaking her in two.

"Forgive me," she whispered, her hips rolling against his hold on her.

He whispered her name as he moved along her chest, his fingers causing friction, her body demanding release. "Come for me, Linzi. Let yourself go and let me feel you grant me your release." He tugged at her breast with his lips, his fingers pressing hard against the material of her skirt against her center.

She hit her head against the house, the world exploding into a thousand tiny stars as fire burst from her stomach and raced up her chest, her moans loud and unashamed.

"That's it," he whispered, his lips pressed to her neck again, his tongue lapping at her as she calmed down. She shuddered in his arms, Erik letting her slide down his body as her feet touched the ground.

His arms pulled her close, the awkwardness she wanted to rouse dying at his control of their combined emotions. He leaned down, lifting her chin and softly kissing her lips, a smug smile on his face. "I've never seen anything more arousing." He closed his eyes, his long eyelashes sending another tremor through Linzi. When he opened them his eyes were bright, his pupils large. "I don't think it's your heart we have to worry about." He kissed her softly before taking her hand and pulling her toward the house. "I think it's mine."

Breathless and still panting, Linzi excused herself to her room, her skirt beyond useful for the rest of the day. Erik promised to start working on lunch as she walked on trembling legs to her room. Part of her expected him to follow her, to finish what he had started and relieve himself of the horrid emotions that must be rushing through him, as they were her, moments before ecstasy hit. How he contained himself was a true attestation to his strength.

She changed into a blue dress, not bothering with panties as they would simply be too hot. She would need to do laundry tomorrow, but wanted to wait until he was gone. Spending whatever time with him while he was still there was her first priority, not that it should be.

You're going to fall in love and have sex with the Viking, and then what? He will break your heart. She sighed softly, walking down the hall and pausing at her father's door, the older man sitting up on the side of his bed.

"Da'!" She walked in and knelt before him, guilt at her depravity pushing her to ask for forgiveness. Never in a million years would she admit to the things she had tasted and done, the hoping for things yet to be done by far the worst of her sins.

"Linzi! You're all right. I thought I heard someone beating on the side of the house. It woke me, which is good I guess. How long have I been under with fever?"

"Only a few days. That was me. I thought you were still lost to the sleeping world, so I was cleaning out a sheet that got messy the other day." She reached up and touched his head, his face pale, but skin cool to the touch. She knew hers was burning, probably bright red at the moment.

"Fever's broken. Thank goodness." He swung his legs over the side of the bed and reached for her to help him.

Erik called out to her and her father's eyebrow lifted. "Is Kenton home?"

"No." She stared down at the floor, her face flushed and guilt riddling her body that a moment ago had been filled with the most exquisite torture she had ever felt. "A day or so ago I found a man injured in the field just outside of the house, near death. The war has reached our doorstep." She swallowed, her mouth dry. "I helped him in here and patched him up. He's a Saxon." VIKING

"A Viking?" he roared. "What the hell, Linzi?" Her father moved toward the door, reaching for his sword as he did.

"Wait!" She rushed to the door, stopping him from leaving his room. "He's not evil! Listen, please," she begged. "He's a servant, near a slave, forced to fight like most of the boys in our village." She straightened and crossed her arms over her chest as if to protect her heart along with Erik. "You'll not hurt him. He's a human as we are. He's been working in the field and protecting me since you lay in darkness." She moved in front of her father and pressed her fingers to his chest, the muscles soft, the sickness taking too much from him. "You will only get yourself killed, along with me."

"I don't like it." He set his sword down but didn't let go of it. "He hasn't forced himself on you, has he?" He tilted his head to the side, trying to read her. "They're savage beasts. Known for killing and raping women, probably in that order." He sighed, his face growing pale with weakness. "How could you bring him into the house?"

"He hasn't, and how could I not? He was dying in the field! What sort of person would I be if I left him there to die?" Tears filled her eyes, but she refused to let them fall.

Her father closed his eyes, breathing in deeply and letting it out. "I don't like it. He leaves today."

"Tomorrow."

"Today."

She stomped her foot. "He leaves tomorrow. He's finishing the field." She rested her hands on her hips as she stepped in front of her father, trying her best to sound like her mother. "I saved your life, and his. The two of you have something in common and you better try and get along. I'll not have you offending him when he's been nothing but good to us. He was hit by arrows from his own men and is suffering the effects of that betrayal. We will not add to it."

"Linzi?" Erik moved into the doorway, his hands lifting as if surrendering. "I'm sorry. I didn't realize..."

"Well, you should have!" her father barked, moving out into the hall toward Erik.

Linzi stepped forward to intervene, but Erik lifted his hand toward her and shook his head. "Sir, I appreciate what your family has done for me. Without your daughter's aid and assistance, I would be but a corpse."

"She should have left you out on the field." Her father glared up at the tall Saxon in front of him, unconcerned with the other man's size. VIKING

"I promise I will be on my way by morning. I would like to spend the afternoon trying to repay your kindness by finishing the planting you need completed in the field."

Linzi walked out and held up her bandaged hand. "I can't do it."

Her father scowled. "Did he do that to you?"

"I did it myself!" She huffed and whipped her hair over her shoulder. That too bothered her father, her wearing her hair freely down. "Erik wrapped and cared for the cut. I did it myself trying to find ways to protect me and you if someone came to harm us. I was on my own, what else could I do?"

Her father flinched at her words.

Erik, sensing the change in the tone of the argument, turned and walked back toward the kitchen. He spoke over his shoulder. "I have everything ready to eat. Come eat, regain your strength and I'll tell you whatever you want to know."

Linzi leaned close to her father as she followed him. "I told you he was a good man."

"Don't you dare fall in love with this heathen Viking! Your mother would roll over in her grave." Her father reached out, wrapping his arm around her shoulder and walked to the kitchen with her help.

"Not sure I can help who I fall in love with, Da'."

He glanced over at her as she shrugged, helping put him down at the table and walking to the pantry.

Erik's gaze raked her body, sharp remembrance of his greedy hands and hot mouth caused a moan to creep up her chest.

She slapped at his arm and growled softly at him. "Behave."

He winked and took a glass of water to her father, his words piercing her need and setting it ablaze. "Never."

Chapter 8

Marcus

It was time to mobilize, the men had grown restless after more than a day of resting along the campsite. The mid-morning air was hot, moisture sitting heavy upon them. Marcus brushed his hand over the top of his head, his hair just starting to grow back. He shivered at the thought of the bugs that caused him to shave it in the first place, his cousin far more insensitive to such things as he. Or at least *he had been.*

Had news reached the palace yet? Had the riders made it to their ships and then on to the king? Would Erik's older brother, Nathaniel, suffer the emotional loss of his brother? Would the queen hide away in mourning in her chambers? She was a strong woman, beautiful and brave. He wouldn't mind having her remain queen when he took the throne, her age no matter to him. She would prove to be the glue that held things together, his own desires sated in the bodies of the maidens he brought back with him from Scotland.

"Why have we not moved up the ranks yet?" Halfdan bellowed. "The day's wasting away and you, Marcus, seem to be enjoying a leisurely morning stroll. Tell me what is wrong with this scene before me." Halfdan stood in front of his tent, his breeches and shoes on, but the rest of him on display.

Marcus turned his head from the sight, the man far too heavy for anything healthy to become of him. "I'm headed that way now, Commander. We'll mobilize and move within the hour. Day after tomorrow we'll take on the Scots just a day's travel north of here, several small towns clustered together with perhaps several thousand people. My scouts have reported everything. It'll be an easy win."

"Then get it done. I'm hungry to claim another victory. The one behind us has grown cold."

Marcus kept his personal thoughts of the man's hunger to himself, walking quickly toward the large group of captains who stood chatting amongst themselves. "Call your men to attention! We pack and leave here in less than an hour. Don't tarry, but work with efficiency. Your commanding king is ready to move!" His voice boomed across the campsite, all of the men turning and watching him. The ever-defiant John's gaze a bit more direct than the others.

A yell of response went across the group and Marcus pointed at John. "You. Come with me." He turned and walked back toward the northern end of the campgrounds.

John's long strides worked to catch up with him. "What is it, Marcus?"

"Commanding General. You'll refer to me as General." He stared down his nose at John. "You tell me. I'm nearly cut in half by my cousin as I have to watch him go mad, and yet you stare at me as if the story goes beyond what I recollect." Marcus swiveled abruptly toward the captain, inches from him. "Is there something you'd like to ask me, soldier?"

John stood for a minute, the dark beard staining his cheeks working to make him look younger than he was. Finally his eyes averted to the ground, his teeth clenched together. He was the most loyal of Erik's supporters.

Marcus needed him on his side. The men might not follow if John did not.

John brought his gaze directly on Marcus. "I cannot see our prince going mad and leaving us. He has been beside us all of these years. I mean no disrespect, I'm not calling you a liar, sir, but the story doesn't reconcile well with the man I know Erik to be."

Marcus sighed, long and meaningfully. "People change in a time of tragedy, John. Do you know that the night we all wanted to go into the city and take a woman into our beds and were threatened directly by him, he disobeyed his own words and went anyway?"

"He did not."

"He did. Ask Halfdan. He was reprimanded, warned to lead by example and not by words alone. He had been slipping for a while. The man never wanted to be a soldier." Marcus closed his eyes and scratched his fingers along his nearly bald head. "He didn't want it."

John's eyes grew big. "He wanted to be king? He was jealous of Nathaniel?"

"Heaven's no." Marcus waved his hand, playing the part perfectly. "The idiot wanted to be a simpleton like you, and your friends before the war. He wanted a piece of land and a woman to make him dinner and breed his sons."

John shook his head. "That doesn't make sense. What man would want for less?"

"One not carrying all his marbles." Marcus pressed his lips tight.

"Then why did he go mad? After we had won the battle? We had every reason to celebrate. We sacked the town!"

"He went mad during it. He left Halfdan's side when he was placed to protect our commanding king. Do you not remember his lot that day? It was not more than a day passed. Have you begun to feel the effects of the fever that washed over my brethren too?" Marcus tilted his head to the side, pseudo concern covering his features as if to convince John of something that didn't exist.

"Me? A fever? No." John touched his forehead as if to reassure himself. "I do remember Erik's task, but I thought he had been relieved of it." John squeezed the bridge of his nose, closing his eyes. "He was more aggressive during the battle than usual, but I figured it was from lack of sleep. And sex. The gods only knew when he had been with a woman last. I always thought he never partook." He shook his head. "You're saying he slept with a woman in Northumbria?"

"He did. He was warned if he strayed from orders once more he would be sent back to Denmark to serve his brother in whatever capacity Nathaniel saw fit."

"And you believe that caused him to snap?" John stroked his beard, not buying it. "Seems so odd to me."

Marcus threw his hands in the air and began pacing. "That, in combination with the battle and his jealousy toward Halfdan! His own father had chosen Halfdan over his own son! Why do you think that was? Because the old king knew about his son's lack of commitment!"

John folded his big arms over his massive chest. "It was because Erik was barely a man. He's grown and always stayed equal to us. He's earned our respect."

"Not true and you know it." Marcus stretched and moved back a few steps. "Regardless of what you think, I'll not have your looks and questions laying seeds of distrust and dissent among the men. Mind yourself, or Halfdan will find use for your head on top of a pole, 'eh?"

"Of course, Sire. I understand much better now." John nodded, hitting his fist over his chest and walking off.

Marcus moved to his tent, pulling his personal effects and throwing them into a small brown sack before the sounds of yelling brought him back into the open air just beyond his make-shift home.

"I've news! Who's in charge here?" The small teenage boy yelled loudly, his high-pitched voice yet to find puberty as it jumped around. Marcus walked toward him, Halfdan nowhere to be seen.

"I'm the most senior officer here." Marcus glanced around. "What is it, boy?"

"News from King Nathaniel regarding the death of his brother, Prince Erik," the boy shouted loudly.

Marcus dragged him into a nearby tent. So the King had received the news. "Tell me, boy!"

"A falcon arrived late last night, Sir, carrying the news. We were alerted at the mid-southern coasts this morning as the sun broke through the clouds."

"Give me the summons." Marcus reached out, grabbing the small paper out of the boy's hand. The child's voice grated his nerves.

It is with broken heart and questioning spirit I heard of my brother's passing. He shall be remembered as nothing but a hero amongst our men. Find the men responsible. If they are British, kill them. If they are Saxon, bring them home so my mother and I might decide what justice is to be served.

Nathaniel,

King of Demark

Marcus rubbed his thumb over the King's seal. "Be gone!" Marcus barked at the boy. He walked by a dying fire of red embers. He dropped the letter into it, watching the flames lick the parchment and air for a short gasp. The evidence left to ashes, he then moved around the camp looking for their commander. He finally found the giant bastard sauntering out from the tent of women, tying his breeches as the tent flapped shut.

"Are we ready to move?" Halfdan gave up on reaching under his belly and opened the tent, beckoning a woman to come out and do it for him.

"Almost. Word has arrived from the castle."

"What is it? Give it to me." He motioned with his fingers.

"The boy took it back with him. I was unsure of who was supposed to keep communication and the lad seemed to be practiced in these things." Marcus kept his face neutral.

"You twit." Halfdan sighed loudly. "Follow me to my tent. Then tell me what it said."

Marcus walked beside the larger man, stopping at the edge of the tent and standing in the opening, his eyes adverted to the men who moved about just outside. Watching Halfdan change his top wasn't on his list of things to do.

"Get in here, boy."

The nickname angered Marcus. He was far from the age of being a boy. "The message was straightforward. The king and his mother are in mourning, their hearts heavy. The king will not send another commander to assist you. He demanded I bring victory to the crown and resolution to Erik's death."

"Yes, well consider it resolved." The older man laughed, the sound cruel and nefarious.

"They want the murderers brought back to Denmark so they might act out the punishment of their choosing." Marcus didn't bother explaining it fully. It didn't matter in his opinion.

Halfdan scoffed, now fully dressed and rather intimidating in his stance. "The deed is done. We've already killed them. They were rogue Scottish men and their arrows left us without a face to place upon the crime. Simple." He wiped his hands against each other as if the matter was finished. "You need to learn to use your head, boy. When I'm king, you'll be my commander. If you can learn how to act like one, think like one, or the next wayward arrow of treachery may pierce your own soul."

Marcus nodded, biting his tongue to hold back a response he might regret later. He bowed his head before walking out of the tent, his actions asking for punishment and yet he could care less. He soon would be the only power anyone would answer to, the Vikings taking land after land as they marched. His rule and reign would be with an iron fist, his desires not that of his predecessors. Uniting the landmass under the benevolent hand of Denmark sounded trite and a waste of time. He would lord them into behaving and paying taxes to the crown, his crown. Their sons would be his soldiers, their daughters his whores.

Halfdan's days were numbered, as were his cousin, Nathaniel's.

Marcus hoisted himself on his horse and saddled up, riding through the men and yelling loudly, "We move. March forward! One day closer to Victory. For Erik!" He grabbed his sword out of his sheath and waved it above the men. "For Erik!"

"For Erik!" The large crowd of men surged forward, a few remaining behind as always to clean up, pick up and mobilize their tents.

Marcus laughed with excitement. Erik lay rotting in a field somewhere, never to be found. Should anyone pick him up and see he was Saxon, they might also wonder why the death blow in his chest held the same symbol. *Because he was murdered by one of his own.* A smile touched his lips, the rightness of such dark actions sitting comfortably on his high shoulders.

He would be king, and anyone who thought differently would fall beneath his boots – or arrows.

Chapter 9

Erik

Linzi prayed over the meal, her father's irate eyes locked on Erik the whole time. Erik bowed his head and closed his eyes, the sweet vision of pressing the beautiful lass in front of him against the outside wall washing over the back of his eyelids. She was divine, so wanting of his attention and yet trying to maintain the purity her mother must have warned her about.

How he wished it were just about sex. He squirmed when her father cleared his throat as if he knew Erik's thought. Sometime that morning, talking to her, he realized how much more he wanted. Could he give up his revenge and just remain here with her? No one would ever know.

"Erik? The prayer is over."

He opened his eyes, smiling at Linzi and letting the expression slide as her father grumbled something about him being a heathen. He didn't blame the old man at all. He'd beat back every scoundrel or —prince or otherwise—who thought to come take his daughter's hand or anything else. "Apologies. I was lost in thought."

"And what does a Viking think about? Killing, rape, stealing?" Her father turned his heavy stare back on Erik, reaching for bread and taking a large chunk of it.

Linzi's cheeks colored crimson, but she held her tongue, making him respect her all the more. She had been smart with him, bantering and freely saying what crossed her mind, but with her father she showed a deep level of respect.

"I suppose a true Viking might, Sir." Erik scraped at the stubble growing on his skin. "I simply want to return to the life I had before forced to join the war." He shrugged, his voice conversational, his expression open and approachable, or so he hoped it as such. He hated lying, but life sometimes didn't give you a choice.

"You still have to answer my question." Linzi stood, walking to gather new mugs and depositing them on the table. She poured them ale and herself a glass of water.

Erik picked his up and took a long drink. "What was the question, Linzi?"

Her father looked up from his plate, his eyes shooting daggers at Erik as if he didn't like the sound of the girl's name on anyone else's lips.

"Where will you go from here? Are you going back to fight..." She paused and wiped her eyebrow with the back of her hand. "To fight my br-brother and the people from these lands?" She ignored her father's comment and continued. "Or will you go after the men who betrayed you?" She sat down beside her father, reaching behind him to rub his back. The old man glanced over at her, his face softening, the love between them more than apparent.

"Men betrayed you?" Her father did not sound surprised. "Why? Did you steal their wives or kill their babies?"

"Da'! Stop it!" Linzi warned him. "You don't know him. He, like anyone, deserves the chance to show his character. I believe him and would welcome him under my roof should I ever have one."

"Show character? If I give him an inch, he shall move a foot! I have one child left with me at home. He takes you, and I have nothing."

Erik reached across the table and touched the older man's arm. Linzi's dad jerked back. "I was not raised by wildlings. Not everyone marked a Viking chose to be as such." He stared down at his plate, the need to put the old man in his position rising up inside of him. He took note from the beautiful creature just across the table from him and bit his tongue.

"Erik, you'll have to forgive my Da'. I'm his only daughter and these times are trying. The Vikings have—"

"Have taken everything." He cut her off, sadness washing over him in waves. "I know. I'm sorry for my part in it. Most of my men fought because if not, their wives and children back home wouldn't be fed." He looked up, swallowing the lump in his throat. "It only takes three days for starvation to kill a babe and a few more his mother."

"Your bastard king should rot in hell," her father spat and stood, grabbing his plate and walking toward his room as if drunk.

Linzi stood, but Erik was already around the table to catch the old man, holding him up and helping him to the bedroom. He assisted him in the bed and let him be, the white-haired fool wanting nothing to do with him, not that he blamed him much.

Erik moved toward the back bedroom, his thoughts shifting from the situation before him to the one pressing against the inside of him. He would have to leave her soon. He had to make right what happened in the camp days before. It was his duty. If someone were willing to kill him, to take him out of the equation, then who else was vulnerable?

He ground his fist into his other hand. Who was it? Who had the balls to murder a crowned prince? *Halfdan.* The commander might not have pulled the string to release the arrows, but he had a hand in it.

Perhaps the bastard had finally pulled together the perfect plan to bring him full into power. If that were the case, then Marcus was in trouble. How far could Halfdan's wickedness reach? Across the North Sea? Then his brother, Nathaniel, was in danger. As was his mother.

Anger burned in his belly as he clenched his hands, his heart aching at the lack of power he held to do anything in the moment. He sat down on the edge of the bed, staring idly to his left where his clothes lay folded in a small pile, his broad axe and the intricate knife his mother gave him sitting on top of them. Linzi must have done that, returned the gift. He reached over and stroked the blade. He would surprise her by leaving it behind when he left.

The thought of not seeing her again hurt more than the treachery of his own men. If he left to do this thing and returned, would she wait for him? Could he take her with him? No. Too many dangers out there. If something happened to her and he wasn't able to protect her, he would never forgive himself. A soft sigh left him as he stood and moved toward the kitchen, his words murmured just below his breath. "When the desires of your heart come within a few feet of you taking them, how do you not abandon everything for it?"

Erik walked to her, sliding in next to her as he wrapped an arm around her shoulders. She leaned in and softly placed her hand on his thigh, his body waking at the mere touch.

"I'm sorry about him."

"Don't be. I would be worse if some Saxon or Scot bastard thought to be in the same vicinity as my little girl."

Linzi shifted, turning to face him, a question on her face. "I never thought to ask. Do you have a wife waiting at home?" Her color paled slightly.

He reached out, taking her hand and pulling it to his lips to kiss her fingertips while he watched her. "No. I speak of a hope for a little girl with long red hair and pretty white dresses in the future." He smiled as she melted before him, her heart so pure, and her desires for the same written all over her. He never should have said the words aloud. It could never happen.

She swatted at him, her expression changing quickly.

He caught her hand, question raising his brow.

"You have yet to answer my question from earlier. I'll not ask again, you brute."

He laughed and turned toward the food, gathering a few more pieces of cheese and a hunk of bread. "I'll go to meet the Vikings in Barthmouth, the town's just south of here, right?" When she nodded, he continued. "We're headed there next." He swallowed, worried his next words might send him out of this house tonight. "I am not just a soldier. I was second in command of the entire Saxon army." He held his breath, waiting for her to hit him again. When she didn't, he continued, his hopes building with each word. "I'm sure most of the Scots and English in Barthmouth will want to take my life, but perhaps pledging my honor to fight alongside them, they may change their mind. I can offer them my skill."

"They won't go with you." Linzi shook her head. "They'll believe you a liar. Not a traitor."

He hesitated, letting the tangy flavor of the yellow cheese roll over his tongue for a moment before continuing. "Then I'll fight on my own. Should I live to see the end of battle, I will need to return home. I've family that needs to know I'm alive and well. Who knows what word has been sent back to them."

"False reports? Can word cross the North Sea that fast?"

"We have the best ships ever made." He heard the pride in his own voice and didn't stop it. "If my brother thinks me dead, he'll want revenge and will most likely do something stupid to get it." He held his tongue, worried he had said too much and she would wonder what kind of power his brother had over the soldiers here.

"My brother would do the same."

"Kenton?" He exhaled the breath he didn't know he'd been holding.

"Yes. He's going to be in Barthmouth."

Erik sat back, his mind buzzing with strategy as always.

"I should go with you, to Barthmouth. We could find my brother. He would believe me."

"No!" Erik stood and wiped his mouth, starting to remove the empty plates as she joined him. He turned to find her standing just behind him, the questioning look on her face causing his heart to swell within his chest. He took the dishes from her and pulled her to him, leaning down to hold her tightly against the firmness of his chest, her softness fitting against him with perfection.

"I think it might be wise for me to come with you." She pulled back, her arms around his neck, her eyes wide with concern.

"No." He imagined what her father would do to him if he took her.

"If my brother is there I can talk to him and perhaps get him to help you. Or at least maybe form a small group of the battalion." Her eyebrows pressed together as she thought. "I could ask my friend Martha to come and stay with my Da' for a few days. How long would we be gone?"

"For you no more than a day. I won't have you anywhere near the danger." *Or my men.*

"It would only take a few hours by horse. We can take yours, but I'm sure you'll need to keep her with you. I can walk back. It shouldn't take me more than a day to walk the journey home."

"Alone?" This plan was suddenly forming too fast. She had control over it. Something Erik wasn't used to. "It's too dangerous."

She stiffened, pulling from his grasp and putting her hands on the sensual curves of her hips. "Yes. I'm perfectly capable of taking care of myself. You haven't been here for the last nineteen years and I got along just fine."

"Damn, you'll be the death of me, woman!" He moved past her, his fingers dragging over the flat surface of her stomach as he walked to the door that would take him outside.

"What does that mean?" She huffed, her face flustered, her grimace causing him to smile despite the worry of tomorrow.

He stopped and looked back at her. "It means that I cannot stop myself from hearing the sounds of your moans from earlier, the feel of you trembling against me." He lifted his fingers to his lips and licked at them, closing his eyes and groaning. "The taste of your pleasure is undoing me from thinking straight."

He opened his eyes, the shock on her face giving fire to his spirit and healing to his soul. "I'm going to work the field until it's done. Tonight you won't leave my bed unless I tell you that you can. Understood?"

She nodded, his words commanding and yet held no power. She knew she could leave whenever she wanted to and he wouldn't stop her.

He yearned to see her give herself wholly to him, to watch her rest in the comfort of letting him give her experience after experience of what he could do to her.

He tugged at the front of his breeches, cursing himself as he walked back down the hill, the sun screaming high above him and promising undue repentance for his wicked ways.

Chapter 10

Linzi

His words left her speechless, his straightforwardness stirring up provocative images inside her head that she didn't even understand until earlier today.

"Linzi!" her father called from down the hall.

She hurried to check on him. "Yes?"

He looked exhausted, but his face stared at her sternly. "Stay inside. Let the Viking work, but you stay in here."

"Da'—"

"I'll not rest if I know you're out there with him."

She sighed. He needed to sleep and regain his strength more than she needed to watch Erik sweat in the hot sun. That image of him working created a pleasant sensation in her belly. She tried not to smile. "I'll stay in. I promise." She helped him lie down and brought him water.

She then worked to clean the house the rest of the afternoon, her gratefulness at having help almost crippling her with emotion as the sun beat down on the land beyond her front door. She made sure to take Erik water a few times, his body covered in sweat, his concentration on his work and not her. She stood and watched him a little longer than she should have the last time, the man of her dreams nothing like she thought he might be.

How would she deal with him leaving? He would stay tonight and she already knew tonight would burn in her memory forever. If her heart was the issue, it was already gone as well. She planned on staying in Barthmouth but knew telling him would only cause trouble. He would force her to stay back, as would her father. She wanted to be near him, and also find Kenton.

Her father lay softly snoring in his room. He would be all right on his own. She would just make sure there was enough bread, cheese, and food to last him. Martha could check in on him too, maybe stay here. Linzi giggled. If Martha only knew she was hiding a Viking in her bed... what would she say?

Forcing her mind to more important things, she considered how to travel to Barthmouth. Their horse would have to stay here with her father. She could ride with Erik. His horse could easily carry both their weight.

She sighed as she wiped her forehead. What if the men who wanted him dead succeeded? Would she be able to return here, marry another and be happy?

She glanced up as Erik darkened the door, a smile on his handsome mouth, his hand extended to her. She let him pull her into the open air of her father's field.

"I finished. I wanted to show you, then I need to jump in the creek." He too had apparently been thinking about tomorrow. "We need to talk with your friend today about coming to stay with your father." He cocked his head to the side. "Are you serious about going with me to Barthmouth to find Kenton?"

"I am." She felt the heat of the sun and closed her eyes, enjoying the moment that seemed to be the calm before the storm. "I need to go into town for bread and milk today. I don't have a dairy cow, so I'll need to find something to trade for it in order to keep father fed and taken care of until I can get back."

"Trade the knife." Erik held her hand tightly in his as he pulled her toward the fields. They stopped in front of the large garden plot, the entire area tilled and the bags of seed empty.

"Did you finish this?" She released his hand from hers, moving around the edges of the large plot, her jaw dropped, her eyebrows high. "How? This would have taken me the rest of the week!"

He grinned, a small wicked smile teasing his lips. "I knew we had little time. No way was I wasting my night being out here."

"You didn't have to finish it, Erik." She said the words but was pleased he had.

He stood in front of her, wrapping his strong arms around her, his lips kissing the tip of her nose before moving to her own mouth. His skin was warm, his muscles trembling slightly from overdoing it no doubt.

"It was the least I could do." He kissed her again.

Linzi leaned into him, her fingers coming up to brush by his lips as he broke the kiss and went in for another. She pulled back, laughing. "Go! Jump in the creek! You start this again and we'll never get out of here." She didn't mind his husky smell at all. She shook her head. "I swear you're insatiable."

"I'm a Viking, woman! Some of the tales are true." He moved past her, popping her soft buttocks as he jogged toward the water behind the house.

She yelped, smiling at him as he disappeared around the corner. She turned to walk up to the top of the hill, sitting down in the shade offered by the large oak tree above her mother's grave.

She reached over and dusted off the tombstone, her eyes filling with tears. "Mum... I'm scared. I think I've started to fall in love." She snuggled in close to the stone, her knees lifting to tuck under her chin. She laid her cheek against the curve of her leg and stared at the Celtic remembrance stone. "He's beautiful and wild, like an untamed horse you might find in the forest." She sighed, wishing the wind would whisper words from her mother. "I believe he'll break my heart, but I can't help myself for wanting to walk to the edge with him. It's the biggest mistake I'm ever going to make, but I don't think I'll regret it."

She let the tears spill down her cheek, wishing so badly her mother was here to confide in and give her direction.

Erik wasn't at all what she expected, but life rarely came in waves of familiarity. It's what made living so great, so grand. She wiped her eyes a few minutes later as she took in the view of the land – her home, her country. She could see why the Vikings wanted it, who wouldn't?

She caught sight of Erik out of the corner of her eye. He was headed back to the house naked, his clothes in front of his crotch as he stopped, too far to really say anything unless he yelled. He didn't see her up on the hill.

She stood and headed toward the house, the handsome beast ahead of her strolling into the house nude as the day he was born. Her eyes drew down to the beautiful curve of his arse, his thigh muscles defined and sensual as well. His body covered in ink. His one shoulder carried some kind of Celtic design and the other a Saxon or Viking Rune type of marking. He was beautiful beyond what she could have ever imagined a man could be.

He paused before going into the house, Linzi almost having caught up with him. He grinned mischievously when he saw her. How he could smile when tomorrow he would be on a bloody path to destruction was beyond her. "The water's cold. No showing you my front less I convince you of false reality."

"You're the devil and you should pray for your wayward soul, Viking."

He chortled and slipped into the house, the smile on his face almost convincing her of her accusations.

She walked in and wiped her face quickly while his back was to her. The tears had dried, but she wanted to be sure there was no trace of sadness on her face. She moved to the cupboard, checking a few things before she headed into town.

Erik caught her from behind, wrapping thick arms around her and pulling her back to his chest, his hair wet and dripping onto her dress. He leaned over and kissed the side of her neck, his hand sliding down the front of her dress over the thin cotton to cup one of her breasts as he growled into her ear. "As much as I don't want this day to end, I can't wait for the night."

He kissed the side of her neck again and she shivered, turning to face him.

"Oh, my!" She pressed her hands to her mouth as he moved back, Kenton's kilt fitting him perfectly. "That is the sexiest thing I've ever seen in all of me life."

He spread his feet shoulder width apart and crossed his arms over his massive chest. "Don't push it. I'm not letting you go to town on your own."

She opened her mouth to protest, but he held his hand to stop her.

"It will be better to look the Highlander part." He tugged at the kilt and grumbled something else.

She didn't have the heart to tell him he would stick out like a sore thumb. He was not local and a handsome man like him in a kilt would only draw more attention. She moved close to him when she noticed mud still caked on the side of his neck. She reached up to scrape it off with her nail and he caught her hand, biting softly into the meat of her palm. She watched him, her desire dancing in rhythm with her heart. "You have mud on your throat. I only meant to get it off."

"It's there for a reason. I need to cover up my rune."

"Rune? I thought..." She waved her hand. "Never mind."

"We believe that when marked as a Viking, the gods of Valhalla give you strength in battle, wits in life and stamina in bed to make many sons."

She let her hands fall from him, her chest suffering from the sudden warmth that coveted her skin. She coughed into her hand, the smile on his lips far too precious to mention. The man knew he was skilled, no need to tell him.

"Are you ready?" He walked toward the door, pausing a moment. "I need to get the knife to trade."

"No, I'll trade my mother's necklace. I'll not have your future son losing an heirloom for a pathetic piece of bread. That's ridiculous."

"Valhalla's rune! You're not giving up your mother's items. I'll bring my axe then." He grinned when he saw her look of dismay. "I always wanted to learn to use a pitchfork."

She rolled her eyes. "You won't need a pitchfork. There's still a large sword. It's really heavy."

His eyebrow rose. "Where? I haven't seen it since waking in your room. Is it with my horse?"

"It's down in the field. After moving you, I had no intention of trying to drag it up the hill and possibly cut a leg off in the process. It's down by the large oak tree at the bottom of the hill."

He nodded and slipped out of the house to get it. Linzi checked on her father, who was sleeping. She shook his shoulder and when he groggily woke up she told him she was going to town for bread. He nodded and was back asleep before she left his room.

She went to her room and hefted Erik's large battle axe over her shoulder. She could just imagine how she looked carrying it. She slipped out into the late afternoon, the sun pulling hard and fast at the end of the day. She untied his horse, making sure her father's horse had water and oats.

Erik took the axe from her and affixed it to the horse. The handsome Celt lifted her up onto the beast. He readily joined her, pulling her back to press himself against her. She rode the horse like a man, refusing to keep both legs on one side. It was uncomfortable and just plain silly in her opinion. Erik didn't seem to mind.

He leaned in, his hand holding tight to her stomach before clicking his heels. The horse took off toward the forest. Erik reached around and took the reins from her, shaking his head. "I hope we have no problems while in town. I can't imagine a

Highlander riding in with a beautiful, brazen woman, Saxon axe on one side and Viking sword on the other."

She leaned against him and closed her eyes as the wind drove her hair flying behind them both, her little world disappearing in a cloud of dust.

The short ride to the town wasn't nearly long enough, the powerful mare beneath them antsy to run more.

Erik spoke into her ear. "I'll have to take my horse for a run tonight if she's going to be ready for tomorrow. Her legs feel dull. She's not used to not running." They slowed as they entered the town, various people milling about doing their evening duties.

Erik slid off the horse and offered his hand to her, catching her as she slid toward the earth as well. He kissed her nose before moving to tie up the animal near a watering trough. He walked beside her and tugged at his kilt again. "This thing is horribly uncomfortable. I think my bits are far too large for something like this. What if I need to sit or the wind blows? Dresses are for women."

She laughed and pointed to the bakery shop. "You'll be fine, I promise. I'm going to stop in and see my mother's best friend. Do you want to come?"

He shook his head. "The less we are seen together, the better I believe. I'll go down to the blacksmith and see how much I can get for the axe. I'll meet you in the bakery."

"Be careful and keep to yourself," she whispered, moving from him and stopping at the door as he whistled to get her attention.

"Don't tell me what to do, woman. That's my job."

She rolled her eyes before slipping into the shop, her demeanor very different this trip from the last. Sara looked up from behind the counter, a large woman standing just before the counter as they chatted.

"Linzi! How's your Da'?"

The other woman turned as Sara introduced them.

"Parsha, this is Linzi. Her mother was my best mate before she passed. Lord rest her soul. Linzi, this is a good customer of mine, Parsha."

"Nice to meet you, girl." The other woman shook Linzi's hand and turned back to Sara, who promised to be right with Linzi. She nodded and moved about the shop, breathing in deeply as she enjoyed the soft light of the fire and sweet smells of treats galore.

"As I was telling you," Parsha continued, her voice growing louder as she gossiped. "They say the entire royal family is in disarray. First the boy dies in the fields in battle, and then the eldest is killed in his bed by an assassin. I'm sure the mother's heart is just broken."

"They deserve what they get, Parsha. Have they not killed a million of our sons?"

"Ahhhh, Sara. It's the turning of the war on our homeland. Dead is dead. You don't have to fight the unliving."

"Perhaps they'll pull back the demon's they've sent over here—"

"What happened?" Linzi stepped up, looking over the counter at Sara.

"It's the Saxon. The Vikings are being punished for what they've done to our country." Parsha lowered her voice to sound more mysterious. "The Prince of Denmark... what's the boy's name..." She snapped her fingers. "Erik! Prince Erik. He was killed on the battlefield a few days back by Scots. Guess they took his body because his mother wants it and it's not to be found. I say good for 'em!"

Linzi stared at the large woman, too shocked to say anything.

"They say Prince Erik was the commander of the Viking Army. Now they say his older brother, Nathaniel, lay dead. Murdered while he slept! Those bloody Vikings will kill each other with no second thought."

Linzi touched her fingers to her lips. Her Erik? Surely not. He had said he was a mere man, a soldier. If he were a king's son... She suddenly realized both women were staring at her. She took a large loaf sitting on the counter. "I'll have money shortly," she mumbled, now wanting to get out of the small, stuffy shop.

"No, dear." Sara watched her carefully. "I've had a great week. Keep it to yourself to buy milk and cheese. You need food, you look as if you've seen a ghost." She tossed Linzi another loaf of bread. "One for the road too. Now run to the butcher across the way. He has some great items on sale too today. Use your money there."

"Thank you." She felt as if she might faint. "Ha-Have you seen Martha? I'd like her to come stay with Da' a day or two so I can visit Kenton."

"I thought you said he was well again."

"He is, nearly. I'm leery to leave him on his own."

"I'll close shop tomorrow. I'd be happy to visit with your father. He's an old friend of mine, too." She smiled, nodding her head. "Get going, lass. Don't worry about your father tomorrow. I'll be there."

Linzi sighed with relief. "Thank you, Sara. Again and again." She was grateful Sara didn't press on why she would visit her brother or if she would be traveling with someone or alone.

Sara waved her hand. "It's nothing your mother wouldn't have done for me."

Linzi slipped out the front door, yelping and almost dropping the loaves as Erik bumped into her.

His large hands took her by the shoulder. "You okay?"

"Ready to get out of here. I hate the village."

"Then I shall whisk you away to your castle on the hill," he joked.

She stared at him, wondering if she should ask him who he really was.

Did it even matter anymore?

Chapter 11

Eric

She stood by the horse as Erik went to the butcher for a few pieces of dried meat. He hadn't needed to trade his axe. Ironically, the blacksmith had been struggling to shape a piece of metal and Erik had helped the man. A few copper coins as payment and he had enough to purchase the food Linzi needed. He glanced at the girl. Her mood had shifted for some reason. He had wanted to push it, but the faraway look in her eyes told him the private matter sat heavy on her. He would ask her later that night as he held her close to him in the bed.

He pulled his bottom lip into his mouth, the desire to take her with him when he left to go home clouding his view. He needed to release her, to leave tonight, and yet he knew he had found the woman he would forever be in search of. He knew he needed to focus on plans for finding Halfdan and his men. He allowed himself a moment longer to think of the fiery red-haired woman who had clouded his priorities.

Strong and bossy, sensual and untouched.

He sighed softly, walking into the meat shop as the tall butcher looked up from behind the small makeshift counter. His white apron looked like he had been fighting battles with Erik all afternoon, his smile did not reach his eyes.

"I need to see what you have in the way of dried beef."

"You're not from around here." The man wiped his hands on the stained cloth around his thin figure.

Erik feigned a rough English accent, thankful Linzi wasn't there to hear it. He sounded foreign, but not exactly Saxon. "Just passing through. Do you only sell your goods to those who live in this area?"

"I'd sell my wife and kids if you had enough money." The guy chuckled, the interaction shifting quickly. "You're not here to pick a fight, are you?" The man picked up a large bladed knife. "Most our younger men have gone to fight the Vikings. That leaves us old bastards to take care of keeping peace. We do that by filtering out trouble before it begins. Saves the back and a day in the bed if you know what I mean."

A forced smile tugged at the corners of Erik's mouth. "Speaking of the bed, I've a beautiful young girl waiting for me, so let's get on with me buying her something to eat, eh?"

"Well why didn't you say so?" The butcher pointed to three different meat sticks hanging from the ceiling. "They're all from the same cow, just various degrees of spice added. I would think mild or perhaps medium would do you well."

"Mild sounds good. I have three copper coins to spend, so whatever that will get me."

The man smiled broader now and stuck the knife into the cutting wood. "That'll get you all three logs of beef. How about one copper coin and I'll throw in one mild log and a quarter round of my finest cheese?"

"Sounds like it should please the lady." Erik tried to keep his voice low and feigned the English accent one of his men had taught him years ago. "Tell me, old man, what news of the Vikings? Are there any updates from the field? How are the boys here preparing?"

"The Vikings are vicious, terrible bastards who care not that all of this land is ours." He paused, shrugging. "Our boys are talented, but our commander died a few days back when trying to help the sea-boys just south of us. I hear they're managing but no sense of direction. There isn't time though. The Vikings never stay down for too long."

Erik took the meat and thanked the man for the information, walking out into the night to find Linzi picking at the loaf with hidden emotion still on her face.

He held up his prize. "Meat and cheese." He suddenly didn't want to stay in town any longer. It felt like there were too many eyes and ears.

She helped him secure everything to the mare before holding his shoulders to be hoisted up. He got on the horse with ease and rode behind her out of town. Neither said anything the entire way home.

Her father met them at the door, pleasantly surprised with the gifts they came bearing. A quick dinner eaten mostly in silence, except when Linzi and her father discussed the harvest and their schedule. Toward the end of dinner she finally pressed the issue of traveling to her old man.

"You want to what?"

"Father, Erik is going to stop this war. He needs to find Kenton to get an update."

"How are we to trust that you won't turn on us?" He looked over at Erik as he lifted his head, taking the last bite of the flavorful beef.

"You don't. I can simply tell you that I plowed your entire field and I'm going to fight against my own men simply because I've fallen in love with Linzi. To betray her would be the end of me. As a man, I'm sure you understand that."

Linzi looked at him, her eyes wide, her lips parted in a manner that caused his body to tighten in anticipation. He needed her father to know.

"And what do you expect me to do about that? Thank you and give you my only child?"

"I don't want your gratitude. I know what my people have done is deplorable and until you want a step in our shoes I wouldn't expect you to understand. I hadn't walked a mile in yours until the last two days and my heart has been forever changed because of your daughter's kindness, her serenity. I will fight against the Vikings and I will win." He looked down at the plate before him, pushing the last bit of cheese around. "I was their commander, my father their king, but no more."

Linzi stood from the table, a soft sound of surprise leaving her. Erik looked up quickly, his heart stopping in his chest. "I'm sorry. I should have told you, but I was stricken with the fact that you would hate me more and I had planned to just go. That was the plan, remember, but now I cannot imagine a world without you."

She turned and raced out the door, Erik standing to follow as her father reached out and pulled him back down.

"Leave her be, son. She's going to talk with her mother. You did the right thing by releasing the information. She needs to know all there is to know about you before making the choice to leave this life and take up yours." Her father lifted his glass toward Erik. "If she's in love with you too, then you have my blessings, but you'd better not give her a life of death and horror as I'm sure you've seen far too many day of in your own." He took a swig of his ale. "By the way, you look like an idiot in a kilt." The corners of his mouth turned upward as he pursed his lips, apparently trying to hide his teasing.

Erik lifted his glass and hit her father's, his heart aching to go after the girl. Surely she would forgive him the transgression. He hadn't known her at all and protecting himself seemed the smartest thing to do. He had spilled the fact that he loved her just before, so perhaps that was bothering her as well. Maybe she didn't feel the same about him?

They sat in silence for a while longer, Erik standing when he couldn't take it anymore. "I have to go find her lest my heart burst from my chest."

"Then go!" The older man sighed, apparently giving up on fighting with young love. "But if she's like her mum, be ready for a fight. That fiery woman never let me live a day without a battle between us. God how I miss it now."

Erik touched the other man's shoulder, leaving him to remember the wife he'd lost, before slipping out of the house, his eyes moving frantically around the field before him. He feared she might have gone into the forest. What if his men were already heading this way? They thought him dead, but what if they were hunting for him?

He stood on the top of the hill where Linzi's mother's grave lay. He could no longer put off hiding in this house. He had never been a coward and he was not about to start now. His wounds had miraculously healed fast, his strength returning. He was not one hundred percent but few could match him as he stood now. He scanned the horizon for Linzi. In the few days he'd been here, that lass had changed everything inside of him. Or maybe she had simply straightened him out. He needed to find her.

He jogged to the creek, slowing when he caught sight of something moving in the water. "Linzi? Is that you?"

"No, it's the monster of the deep who eats men's bits and steals their souls. Of course it's me."

He chuckled, the woman never ceasing to amaze him. He moved down to the edge of the water, the bank littered with her small dress. "You're not angry?" He pulled his shirt over his head and then untied the kilt, happy to be free of the itchy thing. The cover of darkness saved him from embarrassing her.

He waded into the water, the warmth lapping up on him as she turned to swim toward him. He didn't hesitate as he reached her, pulling her flush against him and holding her tightly, his hand stretched across the thin stretch of her lower back, large breasts pressed tightly to his chest.

He stared at the beautiful rose etching over her shoulder and covering part of her breast as it disappeared into the water. He wondered how far the ink detail went. He blinked and forced his eyes upon hers. "Apologies. I should have told you."

"You should have." Her back tightened, not from his touch but from the pressure of his words.

"I'd just been stabbed in the chest with two arrows! I didn't know who to trust. I did not know you would take possession of my body and steal my heart in one day."

Linzi cut him off with her lips pressing urgently into his.

He pulled her tighter against him, one hand moving down to cup the soft flesh of her bottom under the water as she wrapped her legs around his waist. He groaned, not wanting to pull from this erotic embrace but needing to speak before desire overcame him. He rested his forehead against her. "Before sunrise I must go. I want to stay here with you, but I can't. I have to fight." He growled and squeezed her bottom in his hand. "How did you do this to me? Are you a witch?" She'd healed his body and changed his soul; it had to be sorcery.

She smiled, but her face remained serious. "It doesn't take weeks or months to know something is right. It takes moments. One look. One touch." She kissed him again.

He wrapped his fingers tightly into her hair and pulled back gently, the action raising her breasts slightly above the water. He leaned down to press soft kisses across the top of them, his tongue licking the rose detail. He would never get enough of her.

She leaned in and kissed along his jawline, his ear and down to his neck, her teeth taking hold at the soft skin along the base of his throat. His hips bucked forward, her soft warmth pressing against his need.

She nearly undid what little resistance he had left. He unlaced her legs tangled behind him and set her feet on the sandy bottom of the creek. She frowned at his actions. "What're you doing? I heard the water would make it most enjoyable."

"You heard wrong." He took a step back, the water barely covering his hips. When her eyes travelled down his body with a look of burning desire, he nearly gave in. "Watch it, woman," he warned hoarsely. "I've little left in me to not take you right here. I want to do this right, but if you throw yourself at me one more time, I'll have you on the grass bank, legs in the air and myself sated. Don't make me regret my actions."

She giggled at his warning.

He, the unkillable Celtic Viking and she was teasing him!

"What did my Da' say when I left?"

Thank the gods she brought up her father! It sobered him – for the moment. "He threatened my life, warned me about your fiery temper and told me I looked like an idiot in a kilt."

Linzi burst out laughing and quickly tried to cover her mouth. "I find you quite handsome in it."

Erik turned and walked out of the creek, giving Linzi full view of his naked body from behind. He grinned when she gasped. He shook the water off his body and wrapped the kilt back around him, thankful the heavy wool material helped keep his erection partially hidden. He turned to face her. "I'll wear it only for you." He smiled at her wide eyes and enjoyed how her chest heaved against the water as she panted. "I'll see you back in the house."

He picked up his shirt and tossed it on his shoulder as he walked back to the house. Warmth spread across his chest, as emotions overwhelmed his system. He wanted her tonight, and always. Would she agree to be his wife?

He would ask her after the battle in Barthmouth. No way was he leaving the young girl a widow if things didn't go as planned. He grinned. Nor would he leave her a virgin.

Chapter Twelve

Linzi

Linzi slipped into the house. She was thankful her father had disappeared inside his room. She didn't want him talking her out of what she planned to do tonight.

She walked toward her room, anticipation for what was to come rolling her stomach into tight knots. She hadn't had a chance to really get into the details of sex with her mum, her being too young and her mother most likely waiting for the right time. That time never came.

Linzi pulled the small towel tightly around her and tiptoed into the room, hanging her dress she'd washed in the creek on the single peg by the door. Her gaze immediately scurried to Erik. He lay on his back, the sheet covering him from the waist down. He was magnificent, the epitome of male seduction. He appeared so casual it made her jealous that he wasn't nervous. The lustful look on his face seemed to also speak of love, but she could clearly see the outline of his arousal and it alone was distracting.

Swallowing hard she moved toward him, her hand gripping the top of her towel so tightly that her hands shook. He reached out, his muscles and tattoos flexing in his arm, his fingers motioning for her to come to him. She stood in fear, worrying at what he might think of her after making love or whether she might be good at it at all. He had been with many women most likely and she couldn't imagine a virgin being the top of his list. "Come here."

She took a timid step and then bent to blow the candle out on the table beside her bed. The dark would hopefully help provide all she needed to maintain her dignity.

He stopped her. "You're going to want it on. I want to see you beneath me, not just fill you. Come here to me. I'll be easy and take care of you." He crawled out of the bed, his body on complete display.

She steeled herself from reaction, instead turning to face him fully and let her eyes travel up and down him slowly as if seduction were a dish she served up often. Terrified would be an understatement for the emotions pounding through her, but she locked her resolve to not show an ounce of fear. As long as her body didn't betray her.

He was far larger than she imagined a man to be, her gaze moving to his handsome face as he stopped in front of her and tugged hard at the towel, a soft cry escaping her as she reached for it. He dragged her in tightly, not allowing her hands to touch anything but him. She looked up as his strong fingers rolled down her neck, holding softly at the base of it and pulling her up to kiss him.

It was soft and loving, his body tense, like hers. She slid her hands over his hips and up his back before dragging her nails back down his back and cupping his arse. The moan from his mouth told her more than words might have, Erik breaking the kiss and leaning down to pick her up, her legs across one arm and back pressed to the other. She covered her breasts with one arm and the junction where her legs meet with the other hand. He smiled down at her, laying her on the bed and crawling to sprawl out beside her.

Ripping the covers from the bed, he tossed them behind him on the floor as she huffed. He laughed and pulled her toward him, Linzi turning on her side to face him. Soft, feather light touches along her side, her hip and thigh caused her to struggle for air. He dragged a finger along her chin, a thumb over her lips as he leaned in and breathed deeply.

"I love the way you smell." He moved toward her ear, a slight tremor running through her. "Tell me your fears so I can remove them."

"I've never done this." There. She bared her biggest fear to him in four words.

He moved back and smiled. "You were made for this, Linzi. Men and women were made to make love, to give each other full access to the ecstasy that together we create."

"Don't make it any easier." She grinned as he turned them, a hunger burning in his eyes as he pressed his upper body to her stomach and legs, wiggling a little to slide in between her legs. She shuddered.

Erik looked up at her before kissing her stomach softly. "Do you trust me?"

"What?" She stared down at him, hoping the shaking inside of her didn't move to her outer body or, heaven forbid, her lips.

"I want you forever, so I ask you – do you trust me?"

Tears swam in her gaze, the fear of disappointing him, the worry over the pain to come, the idea of loving him already and him leaving, spilling over. She laid her head back against the pillow, whispering her response, "With everything."

"Then reach above you and slide your hands around the bars of your headboard. For now."

"Why?"

"Trust me."

She lifted her arms, her breasts jutting out slightly as she tried to breathe. The action made her feel vulnerable, open and willing to let him lord over her. Her thoughts faded into nothingness as his tongue touched her hip bone, a soft whimper leaving her lips.

"I'm going to memorize every inch of your body and make sure you're begging to enjoy mine." His words came out husky, his accent thicker than she had ever noticed before.

She nodded, her eyes wide as she looked down at him. He moved to his knees, his eyes filled with foreign emotion as he brushed his nose along the inside of her thigh, nudging her to open her legs further for him. Her eyes closed again, unable to handle the sight of him scorching her skin with the look of an animal.

"So beautiful. How could I have been given a chance to love an angel?" His words washed over her, his mouth moving up her thigh. Her back arched, a loud groan leaving her mouth, her hands gripping the wood above her so hard the bed shifted. She pressed her lips tight, terrified she would wake her father and have him rush in, sword in hand.

Erik gripped her thighs, his mouth and fingers loving her in a way she had never been taught possible. Unable to help herself, she rolled her hips, small moans from her mixing with the deep low groans from him as the bed rocked with his efforts. Her eyes fluttered, her ability to reason lost to the passion he provided. A deep breath entered her lungs as she clenched, her body lifting, hands moving from the bed to dig into his shoulders, holding him tight against her as hot fire rushed along her veins and scorched her with release.

He drove her past the point of breaking, her body running hard and fast with him toward another one as he continued to lap at her, his hands pulling and tugging as if she were his last drink of water. She pushed at the crown of his head, Erik moving back and looking up, his tongue brushing across his lips.

"No more lest you kill me with pleasure," she whispered, her hands clawing at the sheet below her as she pulled at it, squirming a bit as he watched. His touch made her feel like Aphrodite herself.

He crawled up her body, leaning down to pull her toward him with one hand, kissing her deeply as the flavor of lust rolled over her tongue. She drank from him, her hands digging into his back and pulling him to lie atop her.

He kissed her once more before licking and kissing at her throat, the smell of sex delicious and strong.

"You will be the death of me, I think," she whispered as he kissed her breasts, her worries of being on display lost to the intimacy of his recent actions.

"I believe it's the other way around, *lass*." He sat up, brushing a rough palm down the center of her breasts, over her tight stomach and through the wetness of her sex. She moaned as her hips lifted, the naughty smile on his lips doing far more to her than his touch could.

He rubbed her legs, his eyes moving across her slowly. "Heaven woman. You are easily the most sensual creature I've laid with. Tell me again that you've not given yourself away and that this gift might be mine."

She reached up and pulled him back down, her legs wrapping tightly around his waist as she leaned up to brush her lips by his ear. "Only if you stop talking and take it."

His breath caught at her sudden boldness, his body pressing to the entrance of hers. He was careful and tender, his motions speaking of lust and need, but controlled and considerate of her own newness to such things. His arms held her tightly, his whispered instructions calming her nerves and relaxing her body against the deep thrusts of his.

Sweat stained the sheets below her, their bodies entwined for what seemed like hours as he made love to her soul, her heart forever his somewhere in the midst of the passionate groans and whimpers, the bites and kisses. He stiffened, his arms locking around her as his hands slid down her back and cupped her rear tightly, his face pressed into her neck as he moved faster, his breathing so hot and movements undoing her resolve to let him go.

He groaned loudly as he let himself go, the sound the most precious she had ever heard. Holding him tightly as he slowed, she kissed the side of his face and reveled in the strange soreness that pulsed throughout her body. Sated and breathing hard, Erik pressed his arms next to her head on the bed and hovered above her, wiping a few strands of wet hair from her face. "I love you, lass. I don't know what tomorrow brings, but I know I want you with me."

Hot tears filled her eyes and she reached up to kiss him softly on his cheeks and lips, too terrified to talk of what tomorrow might bring.

Chapter 13

Linzi

The early signs of pre-morning filtered into the room from the small window at the top of her room, her body deliciously sore, her heart on fire for the sleeping giant beside her. He lay on his stomach, his face turned toward her, breathing soft and steady. Linzi turned on her side, excitement causing her heart to race at the thought of belonging to someone forever.

She reached over, careful to not wake him as her fingers moved down the curve of his back muscles, ebbs and flows making up the movement of his hard body. A soft sigh left her, the desire for more of last night causing her body to tighten. Was lust like this?

After one taste of it, all you wanted was more? Would it consume you if you weren't careful?

A soft knock sounded from outside the house. Linzi sat up carefully and slipped from the bed. Someone was at the front door from what she could tell. Sara? If so, she was incredibly early from where the sun had yet to rise beyond Linzi's small window.

She pulled on her nightgown and tugged her hair into a loose knot as she slipped from her room, closing the door behind her and stopping only to shut her father's door as well. The knock resounded again and she grumbled, walking faster. "Hold on."

She pulled the door open, half hiding behind, too aware of her gown being nearly transparent.

A man stood just outside the door. In the dimness of pre-morning she did not recognize who it was. Her heart stuttered. "Kenton?" But why would he knock?

"Linzi!"

The young man stepped forward, a soft smile on his lips, his hair a little longer, his eyes rimmed with dark circles.

"Luke!" She opened the door wider and looked behind him. "Where's Kenton?" Fear gripped her insides in a way she had only experienced once before as a child – when Da' told her Mum had died.

Luke held out his hands. "He's okay. Oh, jeez, I never thought..." He glanced up at the sky just beginning to lighten faintly. "He's back at camp. My mother has fallen ill, I have leave to come home and say goodbye to her." His eyes travelled down her nightgown.

Linzi crossed her arms over her chest, too aware of how the candle from inside the house must be silhouetting her body. She suddenly worried that Luke might be able to tell she was no longer a virgin. Could he notice she had been with a man? She quickly moved back into the house as he followed her.

"I'm so sorry to hear that. Da' had it too." She knew she was talking fast. She tried unsuccessfully to slow it down. "There's a medicine to cure it. You have to trade with the witch-doctor at the edge of town. Da's nearly well again. He took sick the day you and Kenton left."

"Thank you, but I think she's too far lost to the illness." He reached out and touched her shoulder, his gaze soft and sweet, but different from before he had left. War would do that to a person. "You look radiant, like a burning star far above us in the sky."

She smiled, not sure how to respond. His sweet words would have wooed her a week ago, now she tried to look everywhere but at him. "Let me go get, Da'. He'll want to know how Kenton is."

"He's well, just so you know." Luke walked to the table, looking over his shoulder at her, like he had never noticed how much of a woman she was.

She hurried down the hall, worry consuming her. What would he say if he knew she had been with another man? How would he react if he knew it was one of the enemy, right under her roof?

Linzi rushed into her room, nearly knocking over the chair by the door in the process.

Erik lay still sprawled out and asleep. Her stomach tightened at the possibility of Erik reacting poorly that an old suitor had come to visit.

She would have to move fast and if things didn't work out as she hoped, she would do as she always did and improvise. She grumbled under her breath as she pulled her dress off the hook and slipped it on. The shoulders and collar were still damp from the wash she gave it last night.

She stepped back into the hall and closed the door to her room quietly. Moving on to her father's room, she gently shook his shoulder until he sat up, snorting loudly, eyes wild.

"I'll kill him." He reached for his sword under his bed and hopped out, his legs wobbling.

When he reached for the wall, Linzi moved in to help steady him. "It's not that," she whispered, nodding her head back toward her room. "Erik's asleep." *In my bed*, she wanted to add but bit her tongue.

"What's wrong, child?"

"Luke's here. He has news of Kenton."

Her father's eyes clouded over, his brow pulling in tight as he nodded and motioned for her to go. "Let me change. You go to him."

She left, returning to the kitchen. She stood silently, leaning against the wall after she had lit a few candles.

Luke watched her. "How've you been, Linzi?"

"Fine." *Sleeping with the enemy.* "Is my brother doing well?"

Luke smiled, running his fingers through his hair. "Kenton's alive and well, spraying everyone with piss and vinegar."

Linzi relaxed, the tension easing slightly from her shoulders. She worked to make a pot of tea, pointing to the hearth. "Start a fire for us and I'll make tea and scramble us all some eggs."

Luke got up and walked to the kitchen, stopping behind her and running his hand along her arms before grabbing the matches beside her and walking to the hearth.

He had never touched her before, surely today wasn't the day he was going to make himself known to her.

"While we have a moment alone, I want to talk to you about something." He leaned over and poked at the wood, grabbing another piece and throwing it in the center of the broken wood and ashes.

Oh dear. Please not now. He was thinner than she remembered, his ribs pushing against his shirt. She sat down on a chair near the table.

"Before I left for the war, I figured perhaps of all of the lasses I had met, you would be the best suited for relationship with."

"I thought the same—"

"Love will come over time," he said, cutting her off. He moved to sit across from her, reaching for her hands. "We barley know each other, but being together and sharing a life with each other will foster that feeling."

She moved her hands back, tugging at her dress a little as she tried to work through how to tell him. "I've found someone else."

Luke blinked several times and then jerked back as if he'd been slapped, his eyes wide with hurt, his mouth a tight line of disapproval. "Who? We're all at war right now." His question poked her the wrong way, his eyes filling with condemnation.

"He was a stranger that fell ill on our land a few days ago. I nursed him to health beside my father and I fell in love with him somewhere along the way."

"For the love of... He's not English, is he?"

She shook her head.

"This war had yet to come to your doorstep. How would he have fallen ill on your land?"

"He was shot with arrows." She stood, feeling the need to do something with her hands.

Luke began to pepper her with questions, his voice growing more aggravated. She turned toward him, ready to cut him off at the knees when her father walked in, stopping and glancing back and forth between the two of them.

"Am I interrupting?"

"No, Sir. Just quarreling over who'll make the eggs. Linzi wins I guess." Luke stood and walked around the table, her father embracing him tightly and then slapping him on the back.

"Tell me about my boy, Luke. Is he alive?"

"Alive and healthy. He's busy running one of the infiltrates. He's mouthy and gained a wee bit of weight, so he thinks he can boss us around." Luke laughed and walked around the table, now ignoring Linzi altogether.

"I'm going to get the eggs," she whispered and walked from the house, moving toward the chicken coop. He was upset, fine. That was understandable, but if he had made a move like he should have before leaving then she never would have looked toward Erik. She was faithful to a fault, but he hadn't. Like all boys playing men he had waved and smiled and hoped that she might simply get the hint. She knew she was fooling herself. Had she made a commitment to him, she still would have lost herself to the Saxon lying in her bed.

She growled, marching with angst toward the back of the house. She ignored the sound of the door slamming and moved into the small makeshift pen they had for the hens, bending over and picking up the three eggs she could see.

"'Ave you slept with him?" Luke's voice caused her to stand and stiffen, her dress too thin for the early morning light now sweeping around her. His eyes moved about her, his own childish expressions fading to anger and entitlement.

"What did you say?" She stalked out, moving past him as her shoulder raked by his chest. He had no right to come to her home and demand anything of her.

He grabbed her arm, pulling her to a stop and jerking her against him. Arms stronger than they appeared, wrapped around her tightly and he glared down at her. "You look like a sated woman, Linzi, not a silly little girl."

She'd have slapped him had he not held her arms pinned against her sides.

"Have you slept with him?" He shook his head as he repeated his question. "There's no chance of me taking you as my wife."

She struggled to pull back from him, her movements causing one of the eggs to fall from the basket and crack on the ground. He didn't seem to mind, his arms not giving her any leeway. "Find another woman to marry then. I'm taken." She wished she had said, *I've been taken again and again.*

"Who is he?"

"That is none of your business," she growled, pulling again. "Let me go. You're being ridiculous! You didn't even make an advance or tell me of your plans before you left. Was I to wait until you returned no matter how long that might be?"

"You whore! You slept with him!"

"Let me go," she whispered through tears, her jaw clenched.

He jerked and released her, his hand instantly connecting to the side of her face with stinging resolve.

She cried out, the other eggs falling and cracking as she lost her footing and fell back on the grass.

"We leave a few weeks and you become a country harlot?"

His words were no sooner spoken and Erik rushed from the house and over to them, the look on his face scaring even her. Linzi tried to get to her feet. "Erik, no! It's fine."

Erik crashed into Luke with a resounding thud. Luke's body lifted off the ground, the power behind Erik's shoulder ramming into his chest catapulting him across the yard. Erik ignored her, diving onto the other male and punching over and over.

Luke made a feeble attempt to get out from under him before passing out. Linzi screamed for her father, the older man running toward the fight.

Erik stood, his feet on either side of Luke. He stepped back when Linzi pushed him away and tried to help Luke. Her father tried to talk sense into Erik, but as soon as Luke woke, he pushed her off, causing Erik to come at him again.

Linzi turned and put her hand up toward Erik. "Stop it!"

Erik hesitated at the sound of her voice.

"He's my brother's friend." She sighed. "And would have been my husband had you not shown up here half dead. Let him have his anger."

"He deserves it." Erik glared at Luke, half-lying on the ground, his face a bloody mess. "Being scorned is sensible. Hitting a woman and calling her a harlot is not. Even I know how to behave in front of a female." Erik looked from Linzi to Luke, pointing his finger. "Touch her again with your hands or your words and I will bathe in the blood of your children. Do you hear me?"

Luke's eyes moved back and forth to each of them. "Whatever, *Viking*." He pushed Linzi's father's hand away when he offered to help him stand. He rose slowly on his own. "I'll tell Kenton you send your love, what part is left of your heart." He stepped back when Erik lifted his fist. "He'll be thrilled to learn of your decisions. He didn't approve of me anyway." He stumbled off.

Linzi's father moved in front of her, touching her chin and examining her face. "He hit you?" The sun peered the tip of its curve over the far field.

She turned her head and touched her cheek. "It's fine. He was just upset."

Erik stepped in front of her father and wrapped his arms around her in a tight hug, his eyes burning with a fire much different from the one she'd seen in her room only hours earlier. His gaze narrowed. "Any man who touches you from now on will die, so be careful with your own words and actions, yes?"

"Of course." She lifted up, kissing him as her father watched.

Chapter 14

Erik

"We eat. Then we leave." Erik shook his hand and wiped it on the grass.

They headed into the house. Erik retrieved his items from the bedroom and then went back outside to check if there were any eggs left. He swore under his breath at the rising sun and the eggs all gone because of the idiot boy.

He went back inside and helped Linzi slice cheese, meat and bread to share for breakfast. She sat down, Erik bringing over the mugs and pitcher of water.

"I've never known a man to assist with preparing for the meal," her father spoke, his tone not condescending, but curious.

"My mother instilled in my brother and myself that we were equal among everyone. She believed that we had no choice but to serve and be served." He shrugged, glancing at Linzi when she chuckled.

She scooted in closer to him when he sat down next to her. "I like this mummy of yours."

He stared at her. This beautiful girl – *no, lass* – beside him left him breathless, a warrior who could slay millions and yet her body and passion left him vulnerable. Erik then looked over at the haggardly older man across the table, his stomach turning at what the man must think of him. "We need to hurry, less we waste the day." He stared down at his food, waiting for the old man to tell him he would be travelling on his own.

"You'd better keep that symbol on your neck covered, son. They'll kill you on sight."

Did the man not know? "I'm taking Linzi with me." Erik set his drink down, lifting his hand as her father began to protest, the woman beside him stiffening. He wrapped an arm around her and looked back at her Da'. "I need her to bring me to Kenton." He nodded at the door. "I doubt that idiot out there is going to be any help."

"Why not join the Scots and fight the Vikings? Follow them to battle?"

Linzi's head shot up at her father's words.

She had looked lost in thought for a moment and Erik would have liked to have asked what she was thinking. Except he had to deal with her father at the moment. Erik nodded at him. "I cannot follow them, nor would they allow me to lead them. I haven't gained their trust. I'll find my way into my men's camp and find who did this to me." He gestured at his abdomen. "I'll make things right. For me and for you. We'll not advance another step forward."

"I don't like it," Linzi whispered next to him, her head leaning against his shoulder. He leaned over and kissed the side of her head, smiling against the sweet smell of her.

"The Vikings have been crippled, someone inside of the camp has poisoned the minds of the men. When this is over, I need to go home to Denmark to update my king and queen on what's happened. They'll only believe me."

"Then why bring my Linzi?" The old man's words were more of a plea than a question.

Linzi moved from Erik, her face paling before him. She reached across the table and brushed her fingers against her father's arm, a sad smile on her lips. "Sara's coming soon and will stay a few days. I'll be home before you know it."

"You're doing this with a clear head, Linzi? Not just... just... for love?"

Erik knew exactly what the man meant. He waited for Linzi's answer, his breath caught in his throat.

"I do, without doubt, love him," she whispered, a single tear dripping down her beautiful face.

Erik reached over and caught it, his heart aching with how blessed he was in the midst of all that had occurred. The road before them would be hard and lined with danger, but he would press forward and get them to the peaceful life they deserved. "I won't let anything happen to her."

"I believe that," her father answered. "Just don't get yourself killed. You can't protect her when you're dead." He extended his hand to Erik. "She's a crown jewel as her mother was. Make sure she's treated as such."

"Of course." Erik shook his hand and stood, reaching to pick up another slice of meat before moving back from the table. "I'm going to the creek before we leave. I'll be quick."

The water was cold, the night leaving the dark liquid to settle. Erik locked his teeth as he slipped into the creek, a soft growl sounded from him as his body tightened, the sensation painful and unnecessary. He washed the smell of her from his body, their night of passion the best he ever remembered having. It was because of the love that existed between them. The sex was delicious, but the promise of her loving him made the difference.

He needed to take care of business and wondered if sending her back to Denmark where he could protect her was his best option. If someone was willing to take his life, then they would most certainly want to take hers. His muscles contracted, his heart picking up speed at the idea of anyone even coming near her. He would massacre the whole damn world to keep her safe.

"What're you thinking? You look like you're ready to explode." Linzi laughed, sitting on the dry part of the rocks beyond the water's edge.

"That damn boy who showed up before. I didn't think I would react so violently, but I've never been in love before. It does crazy things to you, I guess."

"As handsome as you are and in all the places you've visited you've never fallen in love?"

"No. Never. This is all new to me as well."

She smiled. "Tell me more of your mother. I like what you've already told me. And you have a brother?" Linzi reached over, picking at a flower next to her. Something hedged at the tip of her memory but she couldn't pick at what it was. She let it be, knowing it would pop up soon enough on its own.

He laughed, slipping under the water and pushing back up, his hands running through his short hair a few times. "Throw me the soap beside you and I'll tell you."

She tossed him the soap as he watched closely. The sunlight pressed against the soft cotton of her dress, the shape of her legs on perfect view, the juncture between them the sweetest thing he had the pleasure of tasting in all of his life. He reached for her, wanting to pull her in and take her again, but she jerked back in time, a laugh leaving her.

"I don't like that red mark on your pretty face. It burns my blood. I will repay that boy for hitting you today."

"I believe he's in worse shape than I am. My brother will thank you I'm sure." She smiled and turned so her good side faced him. "What's your brother's name?"

"Nathaniel. I was named after my father; he was named after our grandfather."

The look on Linzi's face gave him pause, her brow drawing in tightly.

"You don't like the name?" He laughed and splashed her.

She scooted out of the reach of the water and crossed her arms over her chest, the motion lifting the soft curve of her breasts above the neckline, his eyes coveting the view. She frowned at him. "Erik. Please tell me you didn't lie to me about being a soldier."

Guilt pierced him. He chided himself internally for not clearing that up yet and tried to work through how to do so now that he was caught in a lie. "I showed up a stranger on your land, an enemy nonetheless. I didn't know you and you didn't know me. I just pulled two arrows from my back, the bowman a traitor to me."

Her eyes moved from him to the ground in front of her as she moved to her knees, her hands covering her mouth. Tears filled her large eyes, his heart breaking at the thought of hurting her.

"It's dangerous to tell you about my family." He moved out of the river, reaching for the dirty towel he found lying on the floor and wrapping it around his waist.

"No," she whispered, pausing as emotion choked her up. Her alabaster cheeks colored red as she let a small sob go.

Erik was shocked by the depths of her worry. "They won't hurt you." He reached for her.

She pushed him back, another soft sob leaving her as she tried to wipe her tears away, as if embarrassed.

He fixed his towel to stay around his waist and took a step closer, hoping that she wouldn't back up again. "I don't understand. What have I done?"

She brushed her hair back, more tears coursing down her face as she closed the gap between them, her arms wrapping around him as she cried harder. He simply held her, unsure of what to do or say, but knowing he would give her anything she desires. If that was to simply let her emotions bleed out on his chest then it was a done deal. She finally stilled, his soft whispers and gentle petting seeming to have worked. "I heard yesterday... in the village... I, I thought you might be, but then I wasn't sure... I should have asked you then. I-I just..." She huffed and inhaled deeply. "Are you the crowned Prince of Denmark, Erik?"

He stiffened, her words stealing the air from his lungs. For so long he hadn't wanted to be a prince at all, but the beautiful woman in his arms deserved nothing less. For her, he would be anything she needed him to. "Yes," he whispered.

"They think you're dead. They think you've been murdered."

"That's a good thing. I will use it to my advantage. One of my own men tried to kill me and if not for you... he would have succeeded." He pulled her up, kissing her mouth as she pushed against him. He let her go and moved back, confusion giving way to aggravation. "What the hell is going on?"

"Your mother must be devastated. Does that not torture your soul?"

"My brother will hold her up until I get back to Denmark. He is her strength and I am her heart. You'll see. Everything will be fine."

She pressed her fingers to her lips, her eyes filling once again.

Sickness stirred in his stomach as he crossed his arms over his chest.

"King Nathaniel of Denmark was murdered in his bed. That's what I heard at the bakery." She inhaled a shaky breath. "They say your queen's locked herself away, both her sons gone and the throne soon to belong to another lineage."

Chapter 15

Linzi

"It's lies." Erik shook his head. "Lies to stir the Vikings and put courage into those fighting against them. Your country is trying to take the upper hand."

Linzi stared at the striking man in front of her. "They tried to kill you. Why not go after your brother as well?" She knew it wasn't a lie, she believed Erik knew it as well. "Who would want to do such a thing?"

Erik's face grew hard. "Halfdan," he hissed. "We need to leave now!" He turned and headed for the house, not looking back to see if she followed him.

Linzi took her time as she walked back. Erik needed space, she knew that without being told. Inside the house, she found a mouth-gaping Sara standing in the kitchen staring down the hall.

Face flushed, Sara fanned herself at the near naked Viking who had just passed. She took one look at Linzi and tutted. "Earl of Hell's waistcoat! You've fallen in love with a Viking?"

Had the situation not been so tense, Linzi would have laughed. "A prince Viking, actually."

Sara blinked, her mind apparently racing. "*The* Viking king?"

"He's just a prince."

"Nay Linzi, if he is who you say he is, he's not the Viking prince anymore. He's the last male of his lineage. He's their rightful king."

"Yer off yer head!" Linzi let the bread she was packing slip from her hands, heat rearing chill bumps along her skin. "Damnit, Sara. You're right."

"Yer Da' said you're going with him." Sara paused as Erik barged through the kitchen and out the door toward the barn.

He looked like the devil's son on a mission to destroy all those in his way. He wore Kenton's kilt over his breeches, his chest still bare except for the axe he carried on his shoulder. His sword and knife lay strapped to his waist.

"Oh my." Sara leaned over Linzi to watch him.

Linzi grinned. "He's quite the sight, 'eh?"

"Lass, he's in everyone's dreams – the good and the bad."

"I hope I can help him." She frowned, uncertain suddenly of the future.

Sara grabbed two loaves of bread she had taken with her and handed them to Linzi to pack. "In a world plagued with darkness such as ours is, you might be the key to the king's salvation."

Linzi numbly stuffed the bread into the bag on the table. The road before them was lined with decisions and hardship. The two of them would not be together. They couldn't be. He would have to return to Denmark, a palace, and the responsibilities of a ruler would never allow him to remain here. Someone had wanted him dead, this Halfdan person Erik had mentioned, and he probably wanted the crown. If a man was willing to kill for it, he would never be a fair and just ruler. He would also never stop until all of Britain was his. "I haven't thought out—"

"Thought about what?" Erik said as he walked into the house, her father moving in behind him.

Sara quickly piped up. "About where you and the girl will stay tonight. A storm's headed this way."

"There'll be tents at the fighting ground, solid strong tents, I'm sure." He took the bag from her hand. "You ready?"

"Give me a moment."

Erik nodded and clapped her father on the back. "I will bring her home. I promise."

"Haste ye back," her father replied. When Erik went outside, he turned to Linzi. "You sure about this?"

"Where he goes, I go." She leaned over and kissed her father. "I love you, Da', always."

His eyes misted but no tears fell. "Say good-bye to yer Mum." He smiled, but the action didn't reach his eyes, sadness sitting like a cloak around him.

"Yes," she whispered and walked from the house, dark clouds hovering along their path out of town. A rainstorm would be welcomed if it could just hold off until they were safe and tucked in for the night.

Linzi stepped off the porch onto her father's land, walking the worn path from her front door to the large stone that hovered above them as if watching over each of them forever. "I love ya, Ma." She wiped the tears from her cheeks and hurried to Erik, who stood waiting by his horse.

The trip to Barthmouth was quicker than she thought possible, her body curved against Erik's, her head on his shoulder as she dipped in and out of sleep. The night of lovemaking left her energy drained, her need for rest overpowering the desire to know more about him. They barely spoke on the ride, both lost in worlds of their own.

Erik shook her softly as the sound of voices rose up around them, the camp busy with preparing for the fight and the upcoming storm. She jolted up, her eyes moving around the faces, some old, but most too young to be carrying the sad weapons they toted.

"Stop." A tall gangly fellow moved in front of Erik's horse, a look of question on his large face. "Who are you and what do you want?"

"I'm Erik the Saxon. The dead prince of my people, and aim to get my revenge on the Viking who took my life. Take me to your leader so that I can pledge my loyalty to you."

Linzi felt her mouth drop. She was now instantly wide awake.

The boy stepped back, his eyes growing wide. Erik pulled his sword from his hip and pointed it at the young male. "Take me to him now or I will prove why the Vikings are winning. It is I who led them the past three years. Now I want to crush them beneath my feet."

The boy tossed his machete, reaching for the reins of Erik's horse and moving him to the edge of the large camp. Men stared and picked up their weapons, but fortunately did not attack. The boy stopped the horse and ran up to talk with a tall brunette-haired man, his back to them.

"Kenton," Linzi whispered and slipped from the horse, Erik reaching to stop her, but she pulled from him and ran toward her brother. "Kenton!"

He turned as shock registered on his strong features. Luke had been right about one thing – war fit Kenton very well. He reached down and scooped her up, hugging her tightly and turning her around once. "What the hell are you doing here? Where is Da'? Is he hurt? Are you hurt?" Kenton patted her arms and legs, a small crowd gathering around them as Erik slipped from the horse and moved in beside her, his hand taking hers as he pulled her back.

Swords pulled from sheaths at his action.

"Kenton, this is Erik. Erik, this is my brother, Kenton." She looked toward her brother, the look on his face menacing, much the same as Erik's.

"Linzi, move back." Kenton pointed his sword at Erik. He nodded at the man standing beside him. "Take my sister. She doesn't need to see this."

Erik stood tall, his arms at his sides not reaching for his axe or sword as Linzi thought he would. "Touch Linzi," he warned the man moving toward them, "and I'll kill every one of you standing around me. Including her brother."

The man hesitated and looked at Kenton for direction.

Erik stepped forward, swords moving closer to him as the men moved around Kenton to protect him. "I mean you no harm, boy. I've come to pledge my allegiance to your cause and to step up and take the reins in the battle tomorrow."

Kenton scoffed. "You want to lead? A traitor of a Viking thinks he can win the battle?" He shook his head and spat on the ground. "We don't need your help. We've given up our lives to fight you bastards. What makes you think we'd just open our arms and welcome you to our side? Have you gone mad?" Kenton laughed. "Take him." He motioned to his men.

Linzi jumped in front of Erik. "Kenton, no. He is who he says. You need him on our side." She moved toward her brother to reason with him.

Kenton pointed his sword at her heart. "What poison has he filled your mind with?"

Erik moved far too quickly for her to take notice, Kenton's sword on the ground and Erik's to her brother's throat, his teeth clenched, his beautiful blue eyes wild. "If you strike her, I will gut you and every man in this camp. I am not just any Viking, but was their commander. I want revenge on them more than you can fathom in your innocence. Take my offer or I will be forced to draw a line in the grass and kill all who do not join me."

Kenton pushed against the edge of Erik's blade, blood running down his neck. It was a scrape, but he didn't retreat. "How in the hell do you expect us to trust you? Your men have raped, murdered women and children and feasted on the dead of our brothers south of here."

"I have never killed a woman or a child and you, young man, have no choice." Erik glanced at Linzi before glaring back at her brother. "You will call me brother when this is over, mark my words." He stepped back and sheathed his sword, his left hand resting on the blade his mother had carved for him.

"Take your knife from him now or put one against me too." Linzi moved forward, pushing in between her brother and her lover. Erik pulled back, his eyes shifting to her and then to Kenton. "You kill him, then you must also take a blade to me as well."

Erik pulled her to him, his face a mask of terror.

Kenton stared at the two of them long and hard. He shook his head. "Come," he said and nodded his head. "To my tent, so we may speak privately." The soldiers around them remained where they stood.

Linzi reached for Erik's hand, unaccustomed to being afraid of her brother. They followed him into a nearby tent where two men stood guard outside.

"Stay here," he told the guards.

Linzi and Erik stepped into the nearly barren tent. Erik glanced around and frowned, he apparently expected something more inside the barely furnished lodgings of the commander.

Kenton grabbed a mug off the makeshift writing table and drank from it. He wiped his bloody neck with his sleeve. "You're nothing but a ghost, a rumor of death, and yet here you stand. How?"

"Someone in my own camp wanted me gone. The only reason I'm alive is because your sister saved me."

Kenton's eyes shifted to her.

She simply nodded, the emotion too thick in the air before her.

"How's Da', Linzi?"

"Well. He fell ill to the fever, but I nursed him back to health, while taking care of Erik."

Her brother moved toward her, pulling her into a hug as she felt Erik stiffen beside her. He kissed the top of her head, pulling her chin to look at him. "This man here... do you trust him?"

"Yes, without a shadow of a doubt."

Kenton nodded and released her. He snapped his fingers and one of the guards stepped inside the tent, a male with a mop of red hair. "Pull another tent together for my sister and show her to it. I don't want her out when the storm starts."

Erik moved in beside her. "She stays with me."

"No, she doesn't." Kenton did not hesitate in his response.

"She does. I won't let Linzi out of my sight. She's staying in my tent or I in hers, however you want to look at it."

Kenton shook his head. "You say you want to fight with us. What are you going to do tomorrow? Take her with you on your horse? She stays here, at camp. Beside my tent."

"She will remain here tomorrow. Or, I believe we both can agree on this, she goes back to your farm." Erik moved to the large table where pewter figures were set up, like toys of a pretend battle. "We need to talk tactics for tomorrow."

"We have a strategy," Kenton responded, his chest puffing out a bit.

Erik glanced over the table. "It's about to change."

Chapter 16

Erik

After ensuring that Linzi had something to eat and a place to lie her head down, Erik walked back through the camp, every eye on him. He was sure a fight would ensue at some point during the evening, which was fine by him. He wanted to prove his skills and test his body's strength. If someone had to die for him to do it, it wouldn't bother him at all. They should be leery and someone should stand up to take his life.

The boy had been right in his anger. Erik was a Viking and killing was at the core of all they did. Ruination had become his legacy, but change was in the air.

He found Kenton leaning over a large wooden table, the map he had seen earlier in front of Kenton old and torn in places.

"Show me where you think they'll be attacking from." Erik stopped beside him, speaking loudly and gaining the attention of others standing around the table.

Kenton frowned, apparently unsure if he should trust the tall, massive foreigner. He sighed. "They'll come up through the Vadula Valley. Your style is to fight on an open battlefield."

"Noted, but you're wrong. Under my command, they would have been straightforward and marched right out to fight fair. Halfdan doesn't play fair. He hasn't a truthful bone in his body. Where I might be a Viking, he's a demon with no heart."

"Is it true that you're Prince Erik of Denmark?" An older male moved toward him, his fingers rubbing his face as if trying to get something off his cheek.

"Why does it matter?" Erik looked up, his hands pressed to the table before him.

"It matters quite a bit. If we take you out there as a ghost who knows a few men, that's one thing. If we let you lead us as the King of Denmark that is quite another."

"It no longer matters. I am who I am. Tomorrow I am a man on the battlefield, as vulnerable to death as you or any other standing here." He looked back down at the map and studied it, wishing he had one of these maps while fighting for the other side. "Kenton is right; they will bring a large group out through the Valley, but it'll be a third of the men, the rest will be split in half and push from the sides when you least expect it, when you think you are gaining ground." Erik pointed on the map to add to his explanation.

"About the time we think we've won." Kenton stood up, rolling his shoulders. "Take heed tonight, Viking. The men in the camp will be very leery about you being here. I have a large tent. You and Linzi will eat with me, and then I'll put a man outside of your tent. I'll not have anything happen to my sister because of you."

"No man will stand outside of my tent. I will protect what is mine. You and your men prepare for the hardest battle of your lives. Saxons don't give two shits about life or liberty. Coinage, sex, power and the honor of killing in battle are their lusts. You are standing between them and several of those desires."

Kenton began to pace. "What are your thoughts for our strategy?" He was obviously beginning to lean on Erik, that or he was beyond desperate to save his men and their lands. "We were originally going to push along the sides, having our archers take out as many of them as possible."

Erik sat down on a large tree stump near the table. "You don't trust me, but if you know what is right, and what will save your men, let me do this: I'll ride out like a ghost and scare all those on the front line. With fear and emotions high, you will be able to cripple them much faster. Your plan will work fine, but begin with mine."

Kenton stopped pacing and looked over the map. "You ride out to tell them our numbers and we are left as dead men." His lips pressed hard into a thin line. "I love my sister, but I promise you this. You cannot have her and them. You play us the fool and I'll have her heart cut out and fed to the wild dogs."

Erik's own heart stuttered at the crazed words. He knew Kenton was bluffing but he couldn't be one hundred percent sure. The man was threatening to protect his people. He had to respect and honor that. "Let me ride out from the side. They will not know if I am with you or against you."

"And then you think these men will come to the center to speak amongst the leaders?"

"I do. They love to slaughter under the false pretense of peace." Erik looked around the faces in the room, trying to memorize each one so he would not kill them on the battlefield.

"And you've done this before? Slaughtered under false pretense?" an older man asked.

"Every time we fight." He stood and stretched. "I'm going to find Linzi. Then something to eat. No man outside my tent and we do this my way tomorrow."

Kenton came and stood close to him, his words only for Erik to hear. "Careful Erik, lest your eyes betray you. My sister appears soft and young, but she is made of steel, her character forged in loss, her heart constructed in perseverance." He straightened and raised his voice. "You'll eat here in this tent. I'll finish with my men. You get Linzi and bring her here."

Erik bit back a remark he only knew would cause trouble. He wasn't used to being ordered around. He could see where Linzi got it from. He nodded and left the tent to find her.

Dinner with Kenton was less than pleasant, Erik keeping to himself as Linzi tried to make conversation between the three of them. He took his leave after finishing his meal, his mind screaming for air, his body demanding his woman beneath him.

"Can I trust you to personally bring your sister to her tent when you are finished talking? I have a sword and axe that need sharpening."

Kenton gestured with his hand, barely acknowledging him. It drove Erik mad but he again kept his response to himself.

He would covet the look on the faces of his men tomorrow. Halfdan would probably shite himself when he saw Erik. The man wouldn't ride out first, he would send his second in command, Marcus. What would his cousin think when he saw him? Would he open his arms or join him in stopping the advancement. If indeed the rumor was true that Nathaniel was murdered, it meant Erik was the rightful king. Nathaniel and all the men, Halfdan included, would have to bow down before him.

If they believed it was him, and not a ghost from Valhalla come to take revenge on their souls. They would be stunned into silence, fear and trepidation rising in their bellies like the great storm that sat above his head. He walked slowly toward the tent they had granted him, grateful for Linzi being with him lest he sleep on the ground somewhere. The men did not know who stood among them, and he was fine with that. Respect was to be. All they knew of him left him at a loss before them, which was fine.

He needed to push his Viking brothers back and then go home to his mother. Her despair was his own for a moment, his eyes closing tightly as he stopped at the opening of the tent and let out a long breath. He needed to get word to her, but he couldn't trust anyone anymore. Would they attack her? Kill her as well and be done with his entire line?

"Shit," he growled, walking into the tent and pulling at his clothes. He was without recourse against them fully until his mother was safe. He sharpened his sword and axe with the stone left in his room, his mind crazed with worry and the pre-night battle rituals he tended to follow.

Finished, he stripped naked and slipped onto the small cot, the bed not big enough for two people. He would have to sleep on his side, Linzi molded around the front of him. He smiled at the thought, the remembrance of her beautiful body against his offering him a thought to take his mind away from battle. She would be his heart, his peace, his everything.

The tent opened as she stepped in, saying good night to her brother. The tent flap closed and she stopped to look at him. Would she always look so innocent, so perfectly in love with him? He leaned on his elbow, rising up to see her as she moved to light a small candle as the day turned into night before them. A loud crash of thunder shot the ground, the lightning lighting up the night over the tent.

He watched her closely, wanting to spout a million words of poetry at her and yet it just wasn't his style. She turned toward him, pulled her dress over her head as the lightning illuminated the room, his breath catching in his chest as her body stood bare before him.

"Thank you for talking with my brother," she whispered in the dark, the sound of her moving toward him causing his heart to race. "I can't believe you are going to fight with our men."

He reached up as she moved onto the bed, ignoring her comments, only focusing on her. "A night without you in my arms would feel like hell. After last night, I never want you away from me." He buried his head in her thick hair. "What have you done to me, woman?"

She let him hold her before speaking quietly. "Promise me you'll protect Kenton. He's not a warrior, Erik. He is a farmer, like me."

He didn't want to explain to her that her brother had changed. War did that to a man. He was a leader now. How he fared in battle would be shown tomorrow. "I will protect him with my life." He took her in his arms, pulling her down. "It's a small cot, so lay on top of me for a while and let me feel you. We can hold one another after I've had my fill of you."

"Yes," her soft whisper wrapped around him, tugging at desire and burning his need to be buried deep inside of her. He helped her into the bed, lying down and coveting the feeling of her body pressed to the top of his, her long hair splayed across his chest and arm. He rubbed her back softly, the subtle scrape of her nipple against his upper stomach causing him to groan. She looked up, the storm giving him another view of her.

"I love you." She moved up his body, sitting up and straddling waist, his hands sliding slowly up the thin column of her ribs and cupping her breasts as he kneaded them.

The sincerity of those three little words shocked him straight through his core. He knew he felt the same but she held a power over him that he would never understand. He grew hard. "I love you too, *lass*." He adored calling her the Scottish term, it felt so foreign on his tongue. "Tomorrow you go back to your father and when this damn thing is done, I'll come to collect you forever." He tried to concentrate on his words, not the delicious pressure of her bare bottom against his erection.

"You promise?" Her voice was thick with desire, the enchanting smell of her driving him mad. She rolled her hips, his hands moving down to help her with a rhythm of his choosing. He pulled her up slightly, shifting his hips to align himself with her.

"When you have me at the cusp like this, I'll promise you anything." He pulled her down carefully, her groan leaving his mind foggy, his body throbbing. He slowly pulled at her hips as she made love to him, her sensual dance the most enticing thing he'd laid eyes on. He pawed at her, rocking against her as she picked up speed in order to bring her faster to ecstasy.

"Fookin' hell," she whispered and quickly covered her mouth, her eyes wide from the rough words she'd just said.

Erik sat up, grabbing the back of her hair with one hand, his other hand wrapping around the curve of her ass as he controlled her completely, his pants in line with the slamming of her tight body against his.

"That's it, lass. Take it. Whatever you need from me, demand it of me, Linzi," he whispered against her neck, the rain pelting the tent and offering coverage for her long groans. She jerked hard against him, Erik taking full advantage of her surrender to him as he moved his hands to her hips, falling back on the bed and elevating his crotch, lifting her up and pressing down as quickly as he could manage it.

The scene before him left him panting, his own stomach tight as he hovered on the edge of losing it. His mind screaming for him to slow and enjoy the girl, his body demanding nothing less than the frenzy he was creating.

She leaned forward, swatting at his hands as he moved them from her and lifted them above his head. "I'm so close. Finish me."

"Say please," she whispered, the press of her hands on his chest leaving him no option as her words hit him like a punch in the stomach. He whispered as his voice left him, air running from his hungry desires.

"Please..." he begged. "Valhalla be damned, please."

She lifted her hips, her breasts just before him as she worked hard and fast, the sound of her efforts pressing down his veins like the darkest wine. He closed his eyes, arching his back and releasing himself, his cry guttural and raspy. He reached for her hips, stilling her as he rocked back and forth, letting her drain from him everything he had to offer.

Pulling her down on his chest he knew without a doubt that he would fight and win, he would return to her and take her to his castle and that if she wanted him to – he would be King of the Saxons.

Whatever she desired... that was his course of action.

Chapter 17

Marcus

Multiple days passed by, their plans being put off by the storm above them. How it could rain so much in this forsaken pit of a country was beyond him. On the second day of the weather, Marcus finally made the call. The next morning come rain or shine they would attack.

The damn fog had returned with a vengeance, the air so thick before them it was almost hard to pull into their lungs. Marcus sat upon his horse, his eyes narrowed as the men were in rank just behind him. He turned to face them, Halfdan on his massive beast just beside him.

"Stay in formation. The English were nothing compared to the Highlanders. They're all made men, untrained farmers, but loyal to their land and families beyond anything you might imagine. Expect a war today, boys."

Marcus moved to view the large Vadula Valley as it stretched out before them. They would march down the center, giving the appearance of being willing to play by the rules. If the stories of their structure and strategy had moved up the coast, then the Scot's would be expecting one large mass advancing forward. Erik had done the same move each time, their girth so wide and strong that they had simply plowed over everyone, but Erik wasn't in charge anymore.

"Do you want me to ride forward when they bring their boy who commands them to stand in front of us?" Marcus looked over at his commander.

Halfdan shuddered. The first sign of weakness Marcus had ever seen in the man. "Make sure you win this. Do it quickly. Your reputation is on the line. And your life. Don't forget that."

"My reputation?" Marcus looked back toward their leader, the older man lifting his brow at him.

"Of course. Are you as good as the slain crowned prince these men march for? Do you have what it takes?"

Marcus knew what Halfdan was up to and locked his jaw shut. He wanted to scream at the portly bastard, to cut his head from his dastardly neck and yet the manly thing to do would be to simply respond and then show all of them. The questions hung all around him, not from the commander, but from the whispers of the men.

Halfdan shifted his horse away from Marcus and yelled to the men. "You'll be under the command of your captain commander, Marcus. Heed his words as you would have Erik's. Fight for your fallen comrade, for your families, for the pussy you'll get tonight. I don't care, but win this. Whatever you want from these shite towns is yours to keep."

The men yelled, the laughter and joking starting.

Marcus yelled a ferocious battle cry, and picked up the marching horn. The men grew silent, waiting for him to blow it. He chose his words wisely before pressing the bone to his lips. "This battle is yet to be won. Save your celebrations and focus. Some of you have prematurely enjoyed a victory that won't be yours, for you will die today. Stay in the moment and leave the future where it belongs." He moved forward about to blow the horn. He squinted into the fog, seeing what his eyes could not depict.

An Arabian Mare moving toward the center of the field carried a hooded figure, the man much more stout than Marcus had thought the leading command of the Scots was. The bastard had moved to the field before he had.

Marcus sent his horse racing to the valley, refusing to not be the first leader there. He rolled his eyes at the Scot's antics, the man's hood covering his face. He pulled his horse short, hearing the angered cries of Halfdan behind him. "I am Marcus! The commander of the great Viking Army. Is it your wish to die today? To let your sons and daughters fall before me and my men? We fight on behalf of our fallen king and prince and we will bathe in your blood to ease our pain. Relent and we will spare some of your men and women." He sat there for a moment, his eyes on the stranger, a sense of trepidation rolling over him.

The figure lifted his hood for only Marcus to see. "Don't ride on my behalf cousin. I'll do that for myself, and as for my brother who was murdered in his bed, I'll find the man responsible and when I do... no mercy will be granted to him or his blood."

Marcus sucked air as if he had been stabbed. "You're... you're dead."

"Then today you shall fight my ghost. May the gods grant me the right to avenge my life." He moved too fast for Marcus to react, Erik swinging something blunt and knocking him from his horse. He hit the ground and rolled, standing as quickly as he could.

His cousin rode toward his men, pulling his hood from his shoulders and yelling loudly for all to hear. "You scorn me, my own men! You killed my family!" Erik screamed, his horse galloping back and forth along the line of men too stunned to move. "You lie in bed with the enemy and bring death to my door. Today is retribution for your actions! I will become the monster you thought me to be! It is my name you'll cry out when I take back from you what you stole from me. History of this day will scream the truth of my lot!"

Halfdan appeared, his face tight and angry. "History will remember you as the Saxon who killed his own people."

Marcus got on his horse, riding toward his cousin as fear tore through his chest, the looks on the faces of his men crippling them before they even began.

"Go home, or prepare to die." Erik's voice wrapped around him as they passed one another, his battle cry bringing out more Scot's than they imagined.

Marcus moved in front of his men, unable to say anything to bring his men back into focus. Halfdan sat on his horse white as a sheet. Lost in his own terror.

"Do not be fooled by the Scots' tricks! Your prince was slain by them! This is an imposter!" Marcus surged forward. "Charge!" The men began yelling behind him as they moved in for battle with the Scots.

He scanned the foreign faces for Erik, searching until he had himself turning in circles. Was he really alive? Did he know Marcus had planted the arrows in his back? Certainly not. Surely he was angry at the deceit and was now willing to kill them all, most likely the evil of their actions spreading to cover all of them in Erik's view.

Marcus finally spotted his cousin, his axe and knife flying into the chests of several of their men, his tactical skills leaving the soldiers dead at his feet. Another group surrounded him, their hesitation causing a few of them to lose their lives. Marcus slid from his horse, pulling out his own sword and axe.

How in Valhalla had he survived? If the bastard was still alive it was time to kill him. If he were truly dead then killing a ghost would be easy.

Other men moved back, not willing to fight Erik. John at the front on the ground, dropping his sword before the dead prince. The battle raged around them and yet the group in the center seemed to have become hidden.

"Erik. Only you can stop this madness." John kneeled before Erik. "We fight for you, my king. We were told you were dead."

"As you can see, I'm clearly not." Erik held his weapons ready, his body ready to pounce.

Marcus rushed through the men standing, forcing his horse through even though the horse whinnied and tried to stop. The horse did not want to be there. Marcus jumped off, sword aimed for Erik's heart. "I told you he's gone mad! He's killing his own men, deranged and deadly." Marcus turned and faced the men. "I command you to raise your weapons!" He spun back to Erik. "Did the arrows from the Scots not kill you, old boy?" Marcus snorted, lifting his weapons.

Erik was the most skilled of all of them, but if Marcus could get in the other man's head, he could bring him down. Surely he still had to be wounded. And he had his men. He was their commander.

"Scots?" Erik scoffed. "I was murdered by my own men, someone from my own camp shot me in the back as I watched the last city we took as it burned to the ground." Erik lunged, the tip of his blade cutting Marcus across the chest, reopening his wound as he growled loudly, pressing his hand to it.

Halfdan appeared beside Marcus, sliding off his horse and moving in to battle Erik. "Go Marcus. This bastard child is mine to put down."

Marcus growled softly, the men around him moving back behind Erik, pulling others with them. Marcus knew the battle would be lost, Erik's presence alone changing everything. This was his chance to let Halfdan fall, to remove another obstacle from the crown. He climbed on his horse and raced from the group around Halfdan.

"Retreat," he called as he moved through the valley, his hand brushing by men as he ran. "Halfdan's the demon who tried to kill our prince. Retreat and we shall regroup with Erik by our sides again. Retreat."

He ran for coverage, many of the men running with him. Marcus turned and lifted his hands in the air as the Scot's moved forward.

Erik lifted his hand for them to stop. "Are you surrendering, cousin?"

Marcus dropped to his knees, wondering where Halfdan was. If he lie dead on the field or had crawled off to hide in some pit of shite. "I wasn't the one who killed you, Erik. I mourned your death more than the others... like a brother. The bastard who called himself the new king lied to you and to us. Finish this and come home." Marcus turned as he moved the men back toward camp, the Scots dropping their weapons and the sudden screams of Halfdan leaving a smile on his mouth. If heaven did exist they wouldn't allow him entrance, but it was better to rule a day in hell than serve an eternity in heaven.

Chapter 18

Erik

Halfdan. His whispers of wanting his own kingdom left nothing to the imagination where his desires lay. Erik spoke a few words to his cousin, a few of *his* men had chosen to ride against their own country. To side with him against Halfdan. He knew where their loyalties lay.

He had purposely let Halfdan live. An arrow near his chest, but not enough to cause death, if treated correctly. He had ridden to the sides and around. Erik knew full well the traitor had gone back to his tents to regroup his men.

The shock and awe on the familiar faces at the front of the line laid balm to his quandary of loyalty. Only a few knew of his assassination, none of them friends of his. They were all fed a lie and to find out who would do such a thing would be his mission. He moved back toward the Scots' side of the battle, some of his men following him. The line drawn in the sand and the most vicious of them left trembling by what was about to occur.

Erik knew this for sure; Halfdan had meticulously planned Erik's death, but he hadn't done it himself. He had tried to make it look like the Scots or English had done it, but the arrows were Saxon.

Not wanting to give Marcus or Halfdan a moment to rectify what had just happened, by explaining it away and soothing their men from the frantic worry, Erik called the Scotsmen to attack. The large group of men around him stood with fury in their eyes and screamed out a victory cry that far outweighed any he had heard before that day. To fight another who wanted to take something that was rightfully yours created a fire inside the inexperienced countrymen that even the mighty Saxon should be trembling from.

Linzi's face slipped into his vision as he gathered the troops and shook John's hand. He hugged his comrade and curtly explained that he was truly alive. The ten men who had left Halfdan's army to follow Erik would prove useful. "You must help hold the line."

He then rode out toward the massive Saxon Army, his eyes moving to the right to ensure Kenton was beside him. Erik would fight and lose himself in killing, but if anything happened to the boy, Linzi would be devastated. John rode on his left. He leaned over to his faithful officer. "Don't let the boy on my right die. I've a promise I must keep." Erik yelled to Kenton just before the wave of Celt's crashed into them. "Watch your arse out here today! I promised your sister!"

Kenton replied, but Erik could only make out a few words, and of those, he wasn't sure he had heard them correctly. "Up yours?"

Erik refocused on what lay ahead of him. The battle. Blood and carnage a language he spoke all too well.

It didn't last nearly as long as he thought it would. The realization that the Saxon's had been duped into fighting him pulled him from his murderous haze. Halfdan stood before him, one of his arms gone from the elbow, the large oaf screaming like a maiden in heat with childbirth.

"Stop that and die like a man," Erik growled loudly, circling him like a lion. The rest of the Saxon had retreated, Marcus pulling them back. Erik would deal with his insolent cousin after.

Halfdan spat, his voice rusty and rough from the screaming he had done. "Your father would never approve of your actions.

You've not acted like a prince, but an idiot." Halfdan sucked at the air loudly.

"I wasn't raised a prince, Halfdan," Erik mocked. "I was raised a soldier, a captain and the leader of a great army." He stopped moving, reaching for his belt and pulling his small blade. "How about I give you a commander's death? Take your own life and I shall spare you the agony of taking you apart limb from limb." He scoffed. "Though it seems we've started that already."

"The Saxon who killed his own men?" Halfdan rose with no intention of going quietly into the night. "What will the stories be told of you, *boy*?!"

Erik drew his sword and nicked Halfdan on his wrist, enough for the old man to drop his sword. "I should think you would be worrying about your own stories, old man. Or the ones they never tell about you. You'll end up forgotten, your bones buried here on foreign soil where the wild animals shite." He raised his sword to Halfdan's neck. "You ordered me dead!"

"It wasn't me."

Erik shook his head. Even now, near death, the man had no Saxon pride. He would sell his own soul to Valhalla itself.

"I tell you no lies. It was your cousin. He has no line to the crown. He took advantage of me as well. I would never have had your brother killed. Are you mad?" Halfdan yelled, swiping at the offered weapon. "I'll not take my own life. I served the crown all my life. Your father, your brother. I deserve something for the years of toil. I deserve this country as my crown."

"That title belongs to me." Erik turned and looked at the Scottish men behind him, slipping the knife back into his belt. "Do you want to see what mercy looks like today, or are you here to take back what is rightfully yours from the hands of these bastards?"

"Are you not the same bastard?" Halfdan pulled his sword and lunged.

A young boy moved in behind Eric and took the blade in his chest, his life crumbling before all of them in an effort to show loyalty to their new commander. Erik screamed and attacked, his two weapons swinging over and over until nothing was left of the scoundrel before him.

He stood and stumbled to the boy, all the Scottish soldiers having moved back during his rage. He dropped to his knees and touched the child's chest, tears filling his eyes. The boy, the one who had brought him into camp struggled to breathe, his body trembling. "You would die for me?" Erik could not understand why.

"I would die for freedom." The boy gasped and began to shake, blood pouring from his wound. "You will be king? You will right what was wronged?"

Erik nodded, unsure of his plans, but desperately wanting the young boy to believe there was good in him, though he didn't know if it were true.

"Then make this stop." The boy reached out, his hand touching Erik's as it pressed to the boy's small chest. He couldn't have been more than ten years old.

"I will. I promise," Erik said hoarsely, his voice raw and his throat clamped in pain. Erik held the boy until he passed and then stood, wiping the tears from his eyes as he walked back toward their camp, his horse moving up beside him and nudging his shoulder. He stopped and scanned the crowds of men.

"Where's Kenton?"

A thin soldier, his head down, his clothes covered in blood, looked Erik in the eye and said, "He's not returned, Saxon."

Erik spun around, bodies littering the fields before them. "Those of you able, look through every body and take their weapons. The Vikings will not come and steal from their own dead. If they try, let us use their own weapons against them."

He blinked and scanned their faces, hoping to find Kenton. Their leader would not blend in with his men. Erik hurried to the field, the carnage countless, the bodies littering the ground before him.

Erik stifled a groan as his heart broke as he fell to his knees beside a body. Linzi would be destroyed and it was his fault. If he wasn't to blame for the boy fighting on his own and leaving his side, then surely the very action of the Vikings attacking were because of him. He was the king now and he had allowed this. He should have called rank and pulled back, forcing them to beckon to his words to leave this land, but he hadn't. His pride had overrun his leadership. He screamed up at the grey sky, his howl echoing through the valley.

His need for revenge had killed Kenton. Nothing else. It was his fault. A promise had been made and he had not kept it. He reached to touch Kenton. His skin was cold, his wound in the chest just below his heart. He had been lacerated with a sword, as if a straw man stuffed for practice fighting. The poor lad had bled out and died alone on the field.

Erik reached over and shut his eyes, closing his own and saying a small prayer to his gods and the one of the Scots' as well. Whoever might be listening that day in the heavens, he hoped to catch one of their ears.

Agonizingly he emptied Kenton's pockets, a small watch with his name carved roughly on the back – probably a trinket Linzi or her father had given him. There was also a purple flower with sharp thorns in his other pocket. Erik had seen them before, they were some kind of thistle. Ironically it had survived the beating Kenton's body had taken and lay unharmed in Erik's hand. He put it and the watch inside his shirt pocket to keep it safe for Linzi.

Linzi. His heart had never felt so heavy. He needed to see her and have her hold him in her arms. Would she hate him when he told her of Kenton? He stood and called two men to carry Kenton's body back to his tent. Then Erik pulled himself onto his horse and rode hard and fast, back to the fiery-haired lass that had stolen his thoughts, his dreams, his heart. He was about to break her heart. Could he even face her to do it? He hated himself, how much more would she hate him?

Chapter 19

Linzi

The week went by with no word from Erik, no note, no letter. He was only a few hours away and yet the storm had forced them to stay inside, the water coming down in dangerous patterns. She had ridden back to her father early on the day the battle had been planned to start. Rain had deferred them, but still... a week seemed too long. No news of Kenton or the others either.

Sara had remained with them for an extra day, something warm developing between her father and the beautiful baker. Linzi had realized the attraction only because of what life had taught her the past weeks. She stood by the open door, the rain finally slowing to a drizzle.

Her father came in and sighed. "Lass, he will return. He's not a farm boy or a blacksmith turned solider. He's a Viking and though I hate the bastards, I'm almost glad Erik is one of them."

She turned and glanced over her shoulder. "One Viking against a hundred thousand like him? Seems like the odds alone would leave him lifeless on the battlefield." Hot tears filled her eyes, the ones she had beat back all week long.

The comforting feel of her father's arms around her should have given her comfort, but nothing would rectify the situation until Erik returned.

The sound of a horse approaching just beyond the door had Linzi pulling from the older man and racing out into the drizzle. Her heart thumped hard in her chest, her body trembling slightly as she ran toward the sound, an Arabian horse riding hard and fast toward her.

Erik straightened his beaten, exhausted body when he saw her. His clothes covered in blood, his shoulders slumped forward subtly as if in defeat.

Linzi cried out and ran harder.

Erik tried to pull his horse to a stop and at the same time slide off the horse. It slowed and he stumbled when he hit the ground, but quickly righted himself to scoop her up in his arms and spin her once.

"I was so scared," she whispered as they stilled, her eyes casted toward the ground. Emotion beat hard against her ability to keep it together. His fingers brushed along her back, the other hand carefully lifting her face toward him.

Nothing could be more heart-stopping, more breathtaking than the warrior before her. Strong masculine features held as a treasure the most demanding yet loving gaze she had witnessed in her short lifespan.

"Valhalla could not keep me from you, *lass*. I would march across all the land and fight every battle before me if it meant getting back to you." He leaned down and kissed her hard, the tight grip of his arms pulling her in and tearing the air from her lungs with their steely hold.

She pressed into the kiss, her tongue sliding past the roughness of his lips, needing to taste him, wanting to show him how badly she wanted him. He picked her up again, growling into the recess of her mouth, his hips pressing forward against hers. The sound of her father's voice only seemed to dim the passion between them, nothing truly able to break it entirely.

Her father moved to stand between them, his frown an obvious dislike to the scene he had just witnessed. "Kenton. The battle. How did it go?"

Erik's eyes betrayed pain. "For the greed of a kingdom without a king."

"Come inside and we'll talk." Her father motioned to get out of the rain.

"I cannot." Erik's eyes flittered to Linzi. "My," his voice broke as he said the words, "My brother's dead, and my mother sits in Denmark heartbroken, thinking the gods have taken the three men in her life. I cannot fathom her pain. I need to go. I have to rectify this situation and step into whatever role she wants me to."

"You're going to become the king?" Linzi mumbled, the lump in her throat hot and thick. If he were to become king then a queen would be given to him for political reasons. He would not be allowed to marry a poor man's daughter from a small farm in Scotland. So this was it?

"I don't know. I must go home." He looked toward the ground, a long sigh leaving him.

He wasn't going to come back. She knew it. The look on his face and the pain in his eyes could only mean one thing. He would not be returning.

She didn't want to lose him. "What happened?" she whispered, hot tingles of terror rushed down her arms. "What are you not telling us, Erik?"

The pain in his eyes appeared on his face. His shoulders dropped. "I'm so sorry. I lost track of him and when I found him there was nothing I could do to bring him back."

"Kenton?" She pushed Erik away when he reached for her arms.

He let his hands fall to his sides. "I'm so sorry. I should have been there, but I was..." He stopped as Linzi's father swore.

"It is not your fault." His words must have surprised Erik, because they shocked Linzi. "Kenton chose his path and Valhalla is stronger today because he is there. We will see him again and though my heart breaks in my chest, I know that another life for him would never have fit him as this one did."

Linzi cried for the loss of her brother, for the loss of Erik and the strength of her father. Sadness wrapped its bony fingers around her soul, squeezing painfully tight until she was forced to pull from the hug, soft pants coming from her.

"I'm sorry I cannot stay." Erik looked like he wanted to run from them. "I need to get home. My brother's been assassinated. My mother is in danger as well." He reached for Linzi and when she didn't come toward him, he let his hand drop idly to his side again. "I'll come back. I promise."

She lifted the hem of her skirt and glared at him. "Stop making promises you can't keep, Saxon." She spun around and stomped into the house.

Inside she leaned around the frame of the house, the wood biting into the back of her dress. She knew he would come inside and gather her into his arms and make everything right. He would come any minute... any second. She looked around the empty kitchen, horrified that Kenton would never return. He was gone. Forever. Now Erik would soon be too. She banged her head against the house and let the sound and pain fill the space between her ears. She didn't want to think, didn't want to suffer. Why hadn't Erik come to her? She blinked when she realized why.

She rushed out the door, Erik nowhere in sight as her father stood by the stable, his features troubled with worry.

"Where is he?"

"He left."

"No!" she screamed. She raced with all her strength through the forest toward the long stretch of land that opened up for his journey toward the sea. Her heart stuttered when he came into view.

He didn't notice her.

"Erik... Erik wait!" she yelled with her hands cupped over her mouth, her long red hair getting in her way as she swatted it back. She ran toward him, no air left in her lungs, but she pushed on.

He paused and glanced up as he turned the horse around. He jumped off the creature when he saw her. His arms gathered her into him as he buried his face into her hair. "I love you. I'm so sorry."

"I'm coming with you."

"No, you're not. Kenton died because I took my eyes off of him. I don't know what is happening at my castle, Linzi, but these bastards don't fight fair. They are assassins and—"

She put her fingers over his lips, hushing him. "I'm coming with you whether you like it or not. I saved your life. You owe me. I never took your knife. You owe me."

A smile pressed against her fingers and he kissed the tips of them, shaking his head. "I'm not having this argument with you. I love you too much to let something happen to you."

"And what if something happens to you? How do I live if you die?"

He pulled her tightly to him, his fingers brushing softly across the top of her rear. "Too much blood sits upon me. I can't handle the thought of any more being my cause." His voice cracked. "I can't have your blood on my hands."

Linzi spoke fast, her eyes moving toward the ground in front of her as Erik walked with his horse and moved to stand in front of her, his grip tight on her arm, his face a mask of concern. "I saw the witch yesterday."

"Who?"

"The witch. She told me you would come and you did. She said, 'Sometimes the truth of character lies hidden beneath the call of duty.' You said those words to me that day in the field. Those exact words."

Erik shook his head, clearly not understanding what she was trying to say.

"She told me yesterday I am with you. I've got me a bairn."

"A what?" His eyebrows pressed together. "What're you saying, Linzi?"

She pulled from him, her hands pressing on the flat surface of her stomach. "She told me I hold your babe in my womb."

"That's impossible to know." He blinked. "She's a witch?"

Linzi nodded. She believed the old woman.

Erik moved toward her. Linzi flinched in fear at his reaction.

His face softened, tears filling his eyes again as he leaned down and kissed her along her face and neck, her cheeks and lips. She reached up and kissed him in return, their motions frantic before he cupped her face and laid one last kiss on her mouth.

His blue eyes stared intently at her. "Now that changes everything."

~ THE END ~

Heart of the Battle Series
Celtic Viking
Book 1
Celtic Rune
Book 2
Celtic Mann
Book 3

Coming June 2015

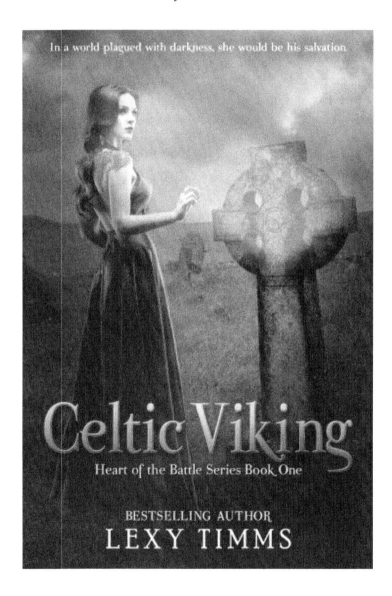

Celtic Rune

Heart of the Battle Series Book Two

BESTSELLING AUTHOR
LEXY TIMMS

Note from the Author:

Thank you for reading Celtic Rune!
If you enjoyed the story, please take a
moment to leave a review on the site you
downloaded the book on so others can
find the Heart of the Battle Series.
I love hearing from my readers so feel
free to connect with me on facebook or
any other social media (you'll find my
links everywhere in the book, lol)
Thanks again,
Lexy Timms

XXX

More by Lexy Timms:

The Saving Forever Series
Part 1 is FREE!

Charity Thompson wants to the save world, one hospital at a time. Instead of finishing med school to become a doctor, she chooses a different path and raises money for hospitals – new wings, equipment or whatever they need. Except there is one hospital she would be happy to never set foot in again, her fathers. He hires her to create a gala for his sixty-fifth birthday. Charity can't say no.

Now she is working in the one place she doesn't want to be, attracted to Dr. Elijah Bennet, the handsome playboy chief, and trying to prove to her doctor father that's she's so much more than a med school dropout.

Why would she try to put together so many things that are clearly broken? Or will she realize in time that they just need to be fixed?

The University of Gatica Series
The Recruiting Trip
Book 1 if FREE!

Book Trailer: http://www.youtube.com/watch?v=5FdSZUaJ2q0
Aspiring college athlete Aileen Nessa is finding the recruiting process beyond daunting. Being ranked #10 in the world for the 100m hurdles at the age of eighteen is not a fluke, even though she believes that one race, where everything clinked magically together, might be. American universities don't seem to think so. Letters are pouring in from all over the country.

As she faces the challenge of differentiating between a college's genuine commitment to her or just empty promises from talent-seeking coaches, Aileen heads to Gatica State University, a Division One school, on a recruiting trip.

The university's athletic program boasts one of the top sprint coaches in the country. The beautiful old buildings on campus and Ivy League smarts seems so above her little Ohio town upbringing. All Aileen needs to convince her to sign her letter of intent is a recruiting trip that takes her breath away.

Tyler Jensen is the school's NCAA champion in the hurdles and Jim Thorpe recipient for top defensive back in football. His incredible ocean blue eyes and confident smile make Aileen stutter and forget why she is visiting GSU. His offer to take her under his wing, should she choose to come to Gatica, is a temping proposition that has her wondering if she might be making a deal with an angel or the devil himself.

* This is NOT erotica* It is a new adult & college sport romance.
For mature readers only. There are sexual situations, but no graphic sex.

COMING SOON:

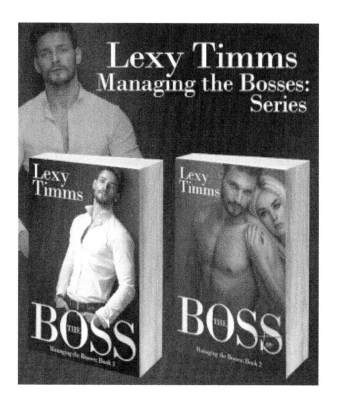

Heart of the Battle Series

Celtic Viking
Book 1
Celtic Rune
Book 2
Celtic Mann

Book 3

Coming June 2015

Did you love *Celtic Rune*? Then you should read *Saving Forever - Part 1* by Lexy Timms!

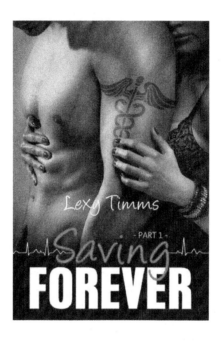

Charity Thompson wants to save the world, one hospital at a time. Instead of finishing med school to become a doctor, she chooses a different path and raises money for hospitals - new wings, equipment, whatever they need. Except there is one hospital she would be happy to never set foot in again--her fathers. So of course he hires her to plan a gala event for his sixty-fifth birthday. Charity can't say no. Now she is working in the one place she doesn't want to be. Except she's attracted to Dr. Elijah Bennet, the handsome playboy chief. Will she ever prove to her father that she's more than a med school dropout? Or will her attraction to Elijah keep her from repairing the one thing she desperately wants to fix? **this is NOT Erotica. It's a love story and romance that'll have you routing all the way for Charity***This is a FOUR book series, all your questions won't be answered in part 1*

Also by Lexy Timms

Heart of the Battle Series
Celtic Viking
Celtic Rune

Saving Forever
Saving Forever - Part 1
Saving Forever - Part 2
Saving Forever - Part 3
Saving Forever - Part 4
Saving Forever - Part 5

The University of Gatica Series
The Recruiting Trip
Faster
Higher

Standalone
Wash
Loving Charity
Summer Lovin'

Love & College
Billionaire Heart
First Love

CPSIA information can be obtained
at www.ICGtesting.com
Printed in the USA
LVOW13s1351220317

528090LV00018B/639/P

9 781512 037128